ForGiving

Dark Tales from the Charity Shop

Tony Hunt

CW01511856

This book is entirely a work of fiction and it refers to some imaginary Lake District towns. The characters I write about in each of the stories bear no relation to any persons living or dead.

'ForGiving' is a charity shop. The people who work here as volunteers find themselves interacting in ways for which their backgrounds and life experience may not have prepared them.

The stories that I have written concern six of these volunteers and a police officer.

THE STORIES

Mickey's Story

'Hello - can you help me, please? There's no size on this, but it looks OK. Would it be all right if I tried it on?'

'Of course! Here, let me show you to our changing room.'

I take the lady into the room at the back of the shop. There, two other ladies are sorting clothes and they smile as the customer comes nervously through the door. I open the curtain for her, and she says thank you to me as I close the curtain behind her.

Five minutes later she comes out of the changing room and to the till where I am standing.

'I'll take this, thanks. It fits perfectly! How much is it?'

'Five ninety-nine, please.'

She gives me a ten-pound note and I ring it through the till. I fold the dress and she places it into her bag; she doesn't want me to put it into one of our own bags.

Thursday afternoon is now my favourite time of the week, starting at one o'clock and finishing by about six. That is the time I spend here on the till. The shop closes at five, but there is cashing up to do, so that's why I said six - just before - as I must catch my bus. I also work on a Tuesday morning, but then it's normally in the back, sorting clothes and tidying up. I know that's important work too, but I don't like doing it as much as I like working on the till - talking to people.

And that's the strange thing - the talking to people - like talking to that lady who bought the dress. I never thought that I would like doing that. I can't do it anywhere else. The people in the house where I have my bedsit - I never chat to them. I don't say anything at all to the other passengers on the bus when I come in to work or when I go home - and some of these are people I see every week at the same time.

There is something about working here that - changes me, gives me more confidence than I have ever had before. Maybe it's the customers. They are very much like me. A charity shop is there for people like me. If you don't have much, you look for bargains wherever you can, and our shop is full of bargains if you know where to look.

Not in the obvious things. One of the ladies who comes in says that tee shirts and kids' clothes are cheaper in Primark - and they are new there! I didn't know that, but I have never had kids, so I wouldn't.

This is the first 'job' I had since I left the army. I was discharged nearly ten years ago - stress, PTSD - and it's taken me a long time to get to this point.

I'm not from around here, I'm what they call an 'off-comer', not local. I'm from North Shields, a Geordie, but when I was being discharged, they asked me where I was going to settle so that they could set up a social worker for me and sort out my travel warrant.

Well, I didn't want to go back to North Shields, did I? I joined the army to escape from there, so I said the Lakes. They said where in the Lakes, and I said 'Winstermere' because that was the only name I could remember, and here I am.

Did you know that Winstermere is not by the Lake? I didn't. If you want to go to the lake, it's a long walk down, and a longer walk back up. That was a mistake - I hold my hands up - and that's one reason why I started looking at Ambleton, and why I work here on a Thursday afternoon - and some Tuesdays.

My plan now is to move here - to Ambleton. I would love to be able to walk to work, and the walk to the lake is easier too. I'd have to get a proper job; I am a volunteer at this shop, but I feel that now I could probably get myself a job - and hold it down. I have been coming here for seven months, and I have never missed a day.

But what kind of a job? I don't want to work in a hotel. I used to be an army chef and there are always catering jobs in this area, but if I never set foot in a kitchen again, it will be too soon.

'Hi - do you work here?' I've been tidying a rack of jackets after a man has tried each one of them on and left the hangers in a real mess.

'Yes, how can I help?'

'I wanted to leave some stuff with you. I'm clearing my mother's house and I thought that these things might be worth something to ForGiving.'

'We are happy to have a look at them. Have you brought them with you?'

'Yes, I'm parked outside.'

'Would you like me to help you?'

'It's all right - It's only a couple of bags. Let me bring them in.'

He thanks me and goes to his car. And he is right, it is only a couple of bags, small shopping bags, at that. I go out to meet him and he gives them to me as, says goodbye and goes back to his car.

And this is typical of my working day here at ForGiving - and I love it! I chat, I serve customers, I help when people drop off things to be sorted, and I help decide what we will throw away. Oh, and I also arrange for all the electrical items that we receive to be sent to our shop in Lancaster because we can't sell them here.

You will think that this is quite ordinary, day to day stuff; it's how people behave towards each other. For me, it is a revelation.

I've never experienced this kind of behaviour before - people being kind and friendly to each other, not seeking to gain any advantage, not wishing to hurt or demean anyone. I have missed all this in the sense of its having passed me by. I have never experienced politeness, never had a relationship where someone wasn't trying to 'win' over me. All my relationships so far seem to have been ones where I had to be on the defensive all the time.

I was in Care until I was sixteen; that was scary and unpleasant. I joined the army and that was the same, if not worse. I got my tattoos to help make me look hard, and when I left the army, I allowed my hair to grow long like a rocker's. I wear bangles and denim shirts and try to look like someone you

2

don't want to mess with.

But the people here don't care. They are mostly older, retired ladies - there is the odd bloke too. But these people don't want anything from me; they are not judging me all the time. And more importantly, I suppose, I don't want to make them feel afraid of me.

'Mickey, would you like a cup of tea?'

'Thanks, Flora. Two sugars please!'

Flora, one of the ladies in the back, has popped her head round the door. She's lovely. I think she's a grandma and I know that she's a retired teacher. She and I often work on the same day together, and she is always friendly.

Now, although she was once a teacher, and I suppose that she stood in front of many classes - Flora hates doing the till! It was she who made me think of working in the front of the shop, handling the transactions.

When I first started, I was in the back room all the time, but after I had helped a couple of customers with their queries, little things, nothing major, she said that I had a talent for talking to people.

I'd never thought this way before. Me? A talent? But I have and working here at ForGiving has allowed me to develop customer service skills that I didn't know I had. And it was Flora who made it all possible.

There's a bus that I get at six o'clock that takes me back to Winstermere. The shop pays my fare because they know that I am on benefits. That's yet another reason why I would like to move here. I don't think it's fair that a charity shop should pay my expenses, but I couldn't afford to come otherwise. Living in Ambleton would be much better for me in all sorts of ways.

I hate where I am now. It's a bedsit, and the other people in the house are all on benefits like me, but don't seem to want to do anything except smoke weed. At least I am trying to do something with my life.

That's my excuse. No, I take that back - what I said. I'm the same as they are - another loser, except that I don't do drugs any more. To tell you the truth, it's all been a bit of a waste up to now. Too many wasted years. I don't have much to show for it - a small army pension, some unpleasant memories and not much else.

But then there's Meg. She is my border collie, and she makes it all worthwhile. She's been my best friend, my only real friend, for the last three or four years. The previous tenant left her here. He nicked off one night, rent unpaid - place in a hell of a mess, and the landlord didn't even know Meg was here.

When he gave me the key to the room, he left me to it. He said that if I wanted to stay I would have to clean the place up. I went to the house to have a look, and Meg was there, curled up in a corner, hiding.

I moved in that morning, didn't tell the landlord about Meg, and she has been with me ever since. I chose her name - I had to call her something, and I have always liked that name.

When I got the ForGiving job, Thursday afternoons and Tuesday mornings -

more if I wanted it, I had to find a way of looking after Meg while I was working, as I did not want to leave her alone. I did ask if I could bring her with me, but they said no. 'Health and Safety', and I accepted that, so I looked around.

Then I amazed myself, and I think that what I did was my first step to getting my confidence back.

Over the road from where I live, there is a young woman who also has a collie, and we used to say hello when we were walking our dogs. A few days after I was offered the job at ForGiving, and completely on the spur of the moment, I asked her if she could keep an eye on Meg for the afternoon. She agreed - straight away. She said that she was sort of thinking of asking me the same thing.

Since then, she - Sophie she is called - takes Meg on the two days that I am working. She hasn't asked me to look after her dog yet, but I would be happy to help her out too.

I don't think that I have ever been happier.

***

I am aware that sometimes people look at me as if they expect trouble. I'm past that swagger stage - the army causes you to behave as if you were a hard man, always looking for a fight, but I'm beyond that. After years of having my hair cut short - even shaved on some occasions, I celebrated my leaving the services by allowing my hair to grow long - and I continued letting it grow - even though I am aware that it's now a bit straggly.

On the bus back to Winstermere last night - on my way home from the shop, I had done a double shift as one of the ladies had been taken ill, a woman tut-tutted me and said that I looked 'shocking'. I didn't reply to her as I was getting off at the time, but as I walked home, I was thinking of what made her feel that she had the right to be so disapproving of me.

I'd bought a few things from the Co-op, and I paid the five pence extra for a bag. I put the shopping on the little table in my room before I went to pick up Meg from Sophie's. I take her for a walk on 'The Rec', a local park where kids play. Then I remembered that I always have a couple of extra plastic bags with me, as Meg sometimes does her business on our evening walk, and when the guy at the Co-op asked me if I wanted a bag, I should have said no, but I wasn't quick enough. As expected, Meg does her business now, so I reach into my pocket for a plastic bag, and out with it comes a little piece of paper.

It is a note! Somebody has written a note and put it into my leather jacket. The note - written, not typed says, 'YOU ARE VERMIN. LEAVE NOW OR FACE THE CONSEQUENCES'.

Meg comes bounding up to me; I have stopped walking and I am standing quite still; she is excited to continue. My mind is racing - who could have written that? Why would somebody - anybody - want to say that of me, or of anyone else, for that matter?

What should I do? It must have come from the shop because that's where I take my jacket off and hang it up when I am working. Somebody must have seen my jacket and it would have been easy for them to slip the note into it.

I forget all about cleaning up after Meg and continue walking. Who? Who could it be, and who was there to be able to do it?

I look at the note again. It is written in Biro, and the paper is white A4, the kind of paper that our printer in the office at the back of the shop uses. I can't be sure, but if it was a sheet of paper from the office, someone who was there - in the back of the shop - must have done this.

My thoughts stop when I hear the voice of a man behind me.

'Hey, are you going to leave that dog muck there? Kids play on this field, you know!'

Another me, maybe the me of ten or fifteen years ago, would have turned on that man and mouthed some obscenity. But not me, not now. I'm not that man any more, but there is at least one person who thinks that I am 'vermin' - there could be more.

I try to laugh it off, 'I'm sorry, I meant to pick it up - here, see! I've got the bag ready and everything. I just...'

I return to where Meg has left her mark and clean up the mess into my little plastic bag. I then walk the thirty or forty yards to where there is a bin specifically for this purpose, and I drop Meg's mess into it. The man has wandered off. He was being entirely reasonable, not angry or pointlessly aggressive, but part of me knows what might have happened if he had tried that on me in my former incarnation.

I know that my appearance worries some people. And yes, I could have my hair cut short, but I happen to like it long.

It will be my tattoos that put people off. A man in a pub once said to me that tattoos were 'Nature's way of telling really stupid people from a distance'. I don't go to that pub now. He and his mate had a good laugh over that.

I have thought of having my tats removed. They were a mistake; now I am the first to admit that they don't look good - especially the ones I did myself. They make me look as if I have been in prison.

It was part of the madness that was Helmand all those years ago. We had so much time when we were doing nothing. A competition developed to see who could get the craziest tattoos. That was the kind of competition I had a chance of winning, and for weeks I would appear with yet another stupid tat that I had managed to force into the little remaining space on my chest or shoulders.

While I was serving, soldiers could have tattoos, but they could not be visible. When I left, I decided that as the army no longer had any control over me, there was space on my arms and hands that needed attention.

Now my arms and hands are also inked - and, of course, I have the regulation 'Love' and 'Hate' on the knuckles of each hand. I also remember being tempted to have a teardrop below my eye - I am pleased that I didn't. These things seem such a good idea at the time, but when you realise that you are stuck with them forever, I'm glad that I didn't go ahead with the tear drop -

or the spider's web over the face!

It wasn't only tattoos in the army. No, on the plus side I did take advantage of their education courses. I became quite literate - I like reading novels and I read good quality newspapers, so in a way I'm a bit of a Jekyll and Hyde character. What you see isn't what you are going to get, but now I'm finding that what people see in me prevents them from getting any closer than they have to.

The combination of my old man's long hair and the tats seems to be too much for some people - it probably has affected my ability to get a job, but to call me 'vermin'? - that's not fair.

I doubt whether tattoos play a large part in the lives of the other people who work at ForGiving, but I thought I had been there long enough for them to be able to see that I am not a thug.

Obviously not! Somebody has a very strong opinion of me, and I would like to find out who that somebody is.

***

You can have tattoos removed for free on the NHS! I have been to the health centre to find out, and I talked to a friendly nurse. She said that she couldn't guarantee it because they are trying not to offer the procedure as it is so expensive. However, in my case it might be possible because of my 'particular circumstances' - she meant my medical discharge, I guess.

All this came out of a chat I had with Sophie. We were out with the dogs a few nights ago, and while we were chatting, she remarked that to begin with, my tattoos had put her off talking to me.

'You do look a bit scary.'

'Why?'

'Can I be honest with you?' Honest? Of course, she can be honest with me. And then she says, 'When I first saw you, I didn't even want to speak to you. I would look to see if you were around before I went out. You look like a criminal.'

'I've never done a dishonest thing in my life.' (Not entirely true. I do have a conviction for shoplifting from a few years ago, but hey!)

'But that's not how you look.'

'So why is it ok to speak to me now?'

'Meg.' That's all she says, that one word. A few seconds later she adds, 'It's when I saw you out with Meg, I knew that you weren't a bad man.' She continues, 'You were so gentle with her; she was a timid dog to begin with, but you have managed to coax some real love out of her. So, when you asked me if I would look after her when you went to work, I was happy to say yes.'

And that's why I went to see if I could get some of my tattoos removed. It wasn't entirely that - my behaviour towards Meg, and Sophie's newly formed opinion of me - but that was certainly the start. I thought that if I could get the tats from my hands removed, and I covered up everything else, that would make it possible for people to see me differently. If that worked, I would decide if a more comprehensive makeover would be worthwhile.

I tell Sophie the next time I see her. 'I've asked about having some tattoos removed on the NHS. I think that they will say yes.'

'That's great news, Mickey!' Then she smiles, 'And when are you going to do something about your hair?'

I laugh that one off, but maybe she has a point. I haven't had many relationships with women in my life, and maybe it's the image thing. I must think about that. For the moment, I content myself with a shrug and a light-hearted laugh. Not enough for Sophie.

'No, listen to me,' she says, 'It would make a huge difference to the way that people see you. It's like you have locked yourself in Time - and it makes you look old.'

And she's right. Apart from the long, straggly hair, I looked much like this twenty years ago. In my civvies, I was a rocker; maybe that was me railing against the army. I am also wearing the same leather bomber jacket I was wearing at that time. I love it; I think that it says who I am. It does - obviously! But in the eyes of other people, it says that I am someone they don't want to know.

But 'vermin'? That word has been nagging away at me.

* * *

Tuesday morning, and this is the first time I have been back to the shop since I found that note in my jacket. I've not told anybody about it; I decided against showing it to Desmond, Mr Blain, the manager, but I have decided to try to discover who wrote it.

The note was handwritten in Biro and in capital letters. I have an idea of the style of writing that this person has, so I will compare it with any examples of writing that I see in the shop.

The best place to begin is the daybook. It's a notebook, always open, and people jot down anything that they think might be relevant to the volunteers who come in for a shift.

Anybody can look at the day book. In fact, we are all encouraged to look at it as we come in, and as soon as I arrive, I start flicking through the pages to see if there is anything that might be useful to me.

There is a lot of spidery, old person's writing! Sadly, there is nothing that directly matches the style that I am looking for, although one or two of the entries do seem to suggest a similarity.

I'm looking at the letters 'E' and 'R', and then I find what I am looking for. Somebody called Joyce, someone that I don't think I have seen before, seems to write those letters 'E' and 'R' in a similar way to the person who wrote the note. I decide to keep an eye out for this Joyce person, and I glance at the rota to see when she comes in to work.

Her name is Joyce Todd and she works on Fridays, and only on Fridays. I have never worked on a Friday, and have never even been to the shop on that day. Yet it is this person's handwriting that seems to be the match I am looking for.

'Anything of interest, Mickey?' Desmond has come in, late as usual, and is taking off his coat and talking into his mobile phone at the same time.

'Hi Desmond. Nope, I was looking - and there isn't.'

'Never is - normally some busybody wants to snipe at me, but it's all good clean fun!'

Desmond is back on the phone - I think it's to his wife. He's right about the sniping. There's a lot of that going on because the volunteers don't think he's doing a particularly good job as manager. He's never around when he should be, is always late for every meeting, and his wife has decided that she is a manager too.

Looking at the day book, I see that there are more entries from her than there are from anyone else. Sadly, each of the entries is a negative one: 'Please don't...' 'Once again, we have found ...' - I don't believe that she understands that we are all volunteers, and not children.

Desmond has changed his mind and has put his coat back on. He is on his way out of the shop when he says to me, 'Mickey, have a look through these price tags. Joyce dropped them off. See what you think. If you like them, we'll maybe start using them this week.'

My annoyance that Desmond seems to be taking another day off is tempered by the authority he has just given me. I am to decide if I like them, and if I like the tags, we can begin using them.

And that's when I see the similarity - Joyce has written them! This is one truly stupid woman, I must say. Her price tags are all capitalised, are all written in Biro - in the same colour and size of writing that was used on the note I found in my pocket. I've got you!

But what to do with this information? I have never worked with this Joyce person; I have seen her once or twice at meetings, and so on. But she is tiny! A wispy little thing. Why could she hate me? I've never done her any harm.

I make a direct comparison of one of her price tags with my note, and I think it's conclusive: she is the one who thinks that I am 'vermin'.

Monica has just come in: I know she doesn't like working with me, and I could have expected something like that from her. But this Joyce person was a surprise.

'Good morning, Monica.' I am polite as usual.

'Hello - er, Mickey.' And she gives me one of those smiles which she uses for people like me. 'You will be working in the back today?' - although it is not quite a question. She won't have to look at me if I stay in the back and she works the till out here.

Could it be her? I look in the day book once again. I try to see if Monica has made any entries into the book, and it appears that she hasn't. I am not surprised; this whole working for a charity thing is beneath her. I don't know why she does it, as she obviously dislikes every aspect of it, and yet she wants to be the next manager. Weird. She has retired up here from somewhere in the

South - doesn't like the locals - definitely doesn't like me.

I redouble my efforts, looking through the daybook to see if I can pin my problems on Monica rather than on someone I don't know anything about.

Nope! Monica hasn't deigned to write a single entry into the book.

I try to strike up a conversation, 'Desmond left some price tags for us to look at. He said Joyce has done them.'

'Yes', replies Monica, she dropped them off on Thursday. Did you not see them? Weren't you here on Thursday?'

I was there, and I say so. I was working on the till. I should have seen everyone who came into the shop. But I didn't see Joyce, or more accurately, I didn't see any stranger go into the back of the shop.

'No, I didn't see her - and I was on the till.'

'Strange. Anyway, she left them for Desmond.'

'He's seen them,' I say. 'He mentioned them to me as he was leaving.'

'Has he been in today?'

'Yes, you missed him by about five minutes.' She smiles that smile again, but this time it is for Desmond. 'He might be back later.'

'Typical!' Monica seems to be annoyed. 'He knew I wanted to see him!' And off she flounces to start her day, a day which will involve her having as little to do with me as possible.

So, it wasn't Monica; I am disappointed. She was on my 'most wanted' list. I could understand it if she had written the note. It would have been consistent.

It was quite a busy day, morning and afternoon at the shop, and when I arrive home I am feeling quite tired. I walk across the street and into the little ginnel where Sophie lives and I knock on her door.

Meg is waiting for me, and after I say hello to Sophie, we wander off onto the Rec for a short walk. Meg loves this time of the evening, and she knows she is going to get a good run around before she has her meal.

It was a few minutes after 7.30 when we get back to my house. In the lobby, there is a small table and an envelope addressed to me. It says 'Mickey'. Nothing else, no stamp, no postal address: somebody has delivered it by hand.

I open it. A single sheet of paper in Joyce's handwriting - I know it quite well by now.

   'YOU SHOULD HAVE HEEDED YOUR WARNING. YOU KNOW WHAT
   HAPPENS TO VERMIN'

***

Thursday morning and I am back at the shop. This time I am not looking for any more evidence. I know it is this Joyce, and I have decided to do something about it. I have spent two days thinking about what I am going to do.

First, I need to find out where she lives. That information is at the shop, on the computer. I have come in early this morning and opened. The keys are at the newsagents down the street; they seem to be open no matter what time I go there.

The computer fires up quite quickly; it's brand new and I was on the half-day course where they taught us how to use it.

I easily access Joyce's address, and make a note of it. It's very near here, just down the street. I close the computer and start to prepare for the day. I am a little early, so I pop out up to the corner of the main road where there is a baker's. I get myself a bacon butty and wander back to the shop.

When I open up the shop this time, Desmond follows me in. He is smiling, 'Hello Mickey. You're a bit early, aren't you?'

'I want to go out to the doctor's later,' I say. 'I have an appointment, but there is a lot of work I wanted to do in the back before I go.'

'You certainly show commitment,' Desmond answers, 'I'm sure that one of the girls could have done the job for you. But at least it will be done well. I do appreciate that.'

And that's the whole point, isn't it? Desmond 'appreciates' the work I do; he asks me to decide about the price tags, and he trusts me to do my work well. This Joyce person needs sorting out - properly sorting out so that I can get back to thinking about my work.

But what should I do? How exactly should I deal with this person who has caused so much anguish in my life? Should I discuss it with her? Should I bite the bullet and inform Desmond about the behaviour of one of his volunteers? Should I ignore it altogether and pretend it hasn't happened? After all, that is the way I have dealt with insults all my life. I pretend that they are aimed at someone else, and I ignore them.

Not this time. I have decided what I will do. I will kill her.

***

Just let me stop you right there! Some notes for a 'would-be killer' - killing somebody is not as easy as you might think!

We are now three weeks on from the promise that I made to myself, but so far, Joyce continues to live - happily, I suppose, although we have not yet met.

She is still spitting her bile towards me, always in the form of the billet-doux with which she excels. Sometimes in the till - on the days that I open up the shop, and of course, once at my house, and that really freaked me out!

The vocabulary has changed, as also have the threats. In one of her notes she promised to hurt me and my family, so she obviously hasn't done any research - I don't have any family apart from Meg, and instead of the word 'vermin', she has graduated to using 'filth' and 'pervert'. 'Pervert' has confused me as sex is never in my thoughts - perhaps too much information, but I have no interest in sex, never have had.

She doesn't know that I have worked out the situation, and that she no longer frightens me. Knowing who my enemy is has taken a load off my mind. I think it's too late now for me to speak to Desmond about it - and anyway, despite the evidence, I am not sure that he would believe me. I have collected all her notes and they are tucked away safely at home. I may approach Desmond - or the police - but now that I am in this train of thought, I want to progress it.

I've let it go so far - three weeks now - because I can't get the killing combination right. If you have a specific person in mind, this equation is important. If you are a nutcase, I suppose that the combination is less important - you might randomly go out and kill on a whim.

But I want to kill one particular person and then carry on my life as normal. I see no reason why I should be inconvenienced by prison, for example, when none of this is my fault. I didn't ask some mad old woman to take against me - somebody whom I have hardly ever met, never spoken to and certainly, never offended. I want my life to be exactly as it was before, but without the notes - and without having to worry if she's been round to my flat. I need to be able to live without Joyce in my life.

So, getting the killing combination right is vitally important, and I am struggling with it.

These are the questions you need to answer satisfactorily before you can kill correctly. Who are you going to kill? How will you do it? Where will you do it? In various ways, these factors need to be carefully considered, and at any given time, one is likely to be more important than the other two. But which one, and how will you know?

The first question, the 'who', is easy to tick off. 'Joyce' answers question number one. The remaining two questions (and I suspect that there might well be more) continue to puzzle me three weeks after I made my decision.

I have thought about killing her in the shop, in her house, surprising her on her way to the shop or on her way back. On her way back would work if it was dark in the evening, but as we are in June, and no solar eclipse is expected, that's a no. Most of the scenarios I have planned involve me getting caught, and we don't want that to happen, do we?

'How' is even worse. Naturally, I have no access to a gun, so that's out. I could obtain an axe or a knife quite easily, but it's the DNA thing that puts the mockers on it. Do you watch those TV cop dramas? If I so much as breathe on her, some trace of me will become apparent. Blood spatter, hair, trace of clothing, fingerprints, obviously - the only way in which I could possibly do it - would be if I wore one of those suits that the forensic science people all wear, and those blue slipper things to cover my shoes. Ludicrous! That won't stand out in a crowd, will it?

'Officer, I have just seen a man in a white forensic suit, wearing those blue thingies over his shoes. He was running away from the scene of the crime. I am sure you will be able to pick him out in the crowd.'

'Thank you, Madam. That excellent description will allow us to do our duty. We appreciate your detailed observations. Good Day!'

Poison! That's a thought. I could keep my distance if I used poison. I'd have to get some first, and I have no idea how I would do that. And how would I get her to take it, seeing that have never met her? Post her a box of chocolates? Invite her round for a cup of tea?

I suppose that I could go for a grand gesture and wipe them all out at the shop - all at the same time! Except for me, of course. That would be silly, and if I am the only survivor, this might cause some suspicion to fall on me.

The plastic bag over the head! I saw that on a video once: it was clean - no blood - and it only needed the victim to be held down for a few minutes.

Joyce is not a big woman. She is bird-like and tiny - but how fit is she? She might be a Karate expert, in which case I'd be buggered. But if she's your typical little old lady, that option would work. I'll make a mental note of that, maybe collect a few plastic bags and test them for their strength. I've got some Co-op bags and I can experiment. I will also need to get a look more closely at Joyce, see her in the flesh so that I can weigh up the chances of success of what I have now decided is my 'method of choice'.

***

Friday is the only day that Joyce Todd works, so I must be in Ambleton on that day. I catch my normal bus, and I get off at the marketplace and walk over to the library to sit there for a few minutes. Rats! It is closed - cuts, I suppose. 'Cuts', the great excuse for nobody doing anything - 'Austerity rules!' - thank God for volunteers like me!

I want to catch sight of Joyce as she goes into the shop. It opens for business at ten. So, any time from now - it is nine fifteen - I can expect Joyce to arrive. Problem is I don't know what she looks like, and I don't want to kill off some random woman because she looks as if she could be a Joyce. I should have thought this through, but as I have never planned to kill anyone before, I feel that I can forgive myself.

I am going to have to go into the shop while she is working and check her out. It would be helpful if I could see her wearing her name badge too - belt and braces - or better, hear someone use her name and see her respond.

I will go into the shop after it opens. I need to think up some reason as to why I am there, and that will have to be a doctor's appointment again. I'm not at all creative in situations like this; I'm sure that a proper hitman would have a believable back story as a backup, but not me. For the second time in recent memory, I will be using the same excuse.

And so, I try it. After wandering around Ambleton for well over an hour - my budget not stretching to even a coffee, as I have had to pay for the bus fare to get me here, I make my way to the shop.

First, I glance through the window. The till is by the window, and I can see that there is nobody standing by it. Then Desmond comes from the back room and moves behind the counter - I can see him as he opens the till drawer and empties the float into it. He does this every day that he is in, and a volunteer, sometimes me, does it on the days when he isn't working. The float is fifty-five pounds, and when it is in the till, we are officially open for business.

We must not have had any customers yet, and that is unusual. It is nearly ten thirty now, and I would have expected the till to have been used by now.

And then I see why. I hadn't noticed it before, but as Desmond moves towards the front door of the shop, I see the 'closed' sign. He opens the door and looks out, and he sees me - I have not had any time to scoot away.

'Mickey! I am so pleased you are here! There's only me here today. I can't get anybody else. I've been ringing around, and then I saw you! Could you work the shop for me - at least until I can get in touch with someone?'

'Yes, I suppose so - I am not on the rota today, though.'

'No, I know,' Desmond looks flustered, 'It's Joyce who would be on with me, but she's not turned in and I can't get a message to her.'

Joyce isn't working today - I have wasted a morning - and a return bus fare! 'Oh, Ok. I can do a few hours if it will help out.'

'You'd be a godsend!' Desmond is delighted. 'If I had known Joyce wasn't coming in, I could maybe have brought Donna with me, but I've got the car, and she doesn't like to walk. I would have to close up before I could go and get her. If you come and man the till, I'll make some telephone calls and get someone in to relieve you.'

'No, I'm happy to help, Desmond. Let's get on.'

We go into the shop and as we do so, Desmond turns the 'closed' sign to 'open' and another ForGiving day begins.

***

A little later in the morning, Desmond comes to me to ask why I am in Ambleton on a Friday. I tell him that I had a doctor's appointment. He says oh, and then he asks me why I don't have a doctor in Winstermere.

I do have a doctor in Winstermere, but I can't tell him that. I say that I am hoping to live in Ambleton, so I registered here. Desmond seems to be happy with that - I would be.

Midday and no sign of Joyce. Monica comes in. She was expecting to be valuing some pottery and paintings today - I saw that in the book - but she agrees to stay on and look after the till.

She is quite stiff with me, formally polite, but I get the sense that she - along with Joyce, it seems - would rather that she didn't have to deal with me. Just before one o'clock I leave. I say goodbye to Desmond, who thanks me for helping him out. Monica doesn't say anything, so I walk around the corner to catch the bus.

When I get back to Winstermere, I see that Sophie is about to take her dog and my Meg out for a walk. I go up to her and say hello, and she looks at me with an expression that I have never seen before.

Is she frightened? Is she embarrassed? I can't tell, but what I can tell is that she doesn't want to go for a walk with me.

'I want to give Meg back to you.'

'Ok. Thanks,' I reply, and then I have to ask. 'Is something wrong, Sophie? You seem unhappy.'

She looks at me. She's not sure what to say. She is looking around as if she is frightened of something - frightened of me.

'I want to go now,' she says. 'Please take Meg.'

I do so. Meg is pleased to see me, and I give her a little cuddle. Sophie walks on, rather quickly, it seems. She obviously doesn't want to be seen with me.

I decide not to worry her further, so instead of walking on to the Rec, where I know she will be going, I take Meg in the opposite direction. The last thing I want to do is embarrass Sophie, she is a lovely person, and I like her as a friend.
***
I get back to my house maybe half an hour after I had picked Meg up from Sophie. A police car is parked just outside my front door, and seeing me, two police officers get out of it.

'Michael Hembrow?' says a policeman. Michael! The last person to call me Michael was my last foster mother, and that was a lifetime ago.

'Yes,' I reply. The policeman continues, 'Do you work in the ForGiving shop in Ambleton?'

'Yes, what's this all about, please. I've just come from working there today.'

'Have you anyone who could look after your dog? We would like to ask you some questions, and we want to take you to Kendal for that.'

I am a bit confused. 'What's all this about?' The policeman asks again, 'Is there someone who can keep an eye on your dog?'

'You could ask Sophie, over the road. It's the bottom flat - the door's at the side.' She is the only person I can think of, but I know that she is annoyed with me; she might say no. The other police officer, a young woman walks over the road to Sophie's.

'Please get in the car, sir,' says the policeman. 'I'll hold the dog.' And he takes Meg from me as he opens the rear door of the car.

A few moments later, the policewoman comes back, signals a yes to her colleague, and she takes Meg from him and walks back to Sophie's.

'Tell you what, as we are here, and before we take you to Kendal, I'd like a look around your room.'

He looks over the road. Sophie is looking at me and she has taken Meg. She must have been there all the time. The young policewoman is returning to the car.

'You'll stay quietly here with my colleague? Let me have your door key, please.'

I think about it, but I can't say no - there are so many things I can't say. My head is bursting! I have not done anything. Yes, I've been thinking bad thoughts, but that is all - thinking!

The female PC stays with me while he goes into the house. She's nervous about this, I can tell, and she keeps looking towards my flat hoping that her partner will return.

He is not in the house for more than five minutes when he returns, quickly gets into the car - he will be driving - turns to me and shows me an evidence envelope. I can see that he has found all the notes from Joyce that I had collected. I hadn't hidden them, they were on my table. He has also brought some plastic bags with him. I collect them - not deliberately, but I always seem to forget to take a shopping bag with me. I know it's five pence, but it's worth it in my opinion.

The policeman continues, 'These notes. Who sent you them?'

He's holding up the evidence bag, 'And tell me about these?' Three or four Co-op bags, 'A bag similar to these that I have found in your room was found earlier today – it had your fingerprints on it.'

His colleague has returned, and he says to her, 'Put the cuffs on him now.'

As she puts the handcuffs on me, the male PC makes it official by reading a statement from a card he has in his pocket.

'I can never remember this damn thing!' he says to his colleague.

'I've never arrested anyone yet, sir,' is her reply.

***

I am in a cell! Me - in a prison cell! I have been remanded in custody for the murder of Miss Joyce Todd of Ambleton.

They sit me down in an interview room to wait, and about an hour after I arrive, a duty solicitor turns up and introduces himself to me.

About five minutes later, two police officers, not in uniform, but CID, and both men, ask me what I was doing in Ambleton this morning at about nine o'clock.

I say that I had come to Ambleton for a doctor's appointment. The younger of the two officers says that's not true - I had also said that to Desmond, but they had checked, and I wasn't even registered with the Ambleton Health Centre.

'Not a good start, Michael,' he says. 'What do you know about Joyce Todd?'

'I know of her, but I have never spoken to her.' That much is true.

'Joyce Todd was a sixty-seven-year-old woman. She was suffocated last night or this morning at her home. The murderer put a plastic bag - a Co-op bag - over her head and suffocated her. That same murderer left his fingerprints on the bag. So, we uploaded them to our system immediately. The fingerprints are yours, and that's why we came to pick you up this afternoon.'

A grenade goes off inside my head. 'I don't know Joyce, and I've never been to her house.'

'Funny how your fingerprints ended up there, then.'

'Excuse me?' I have not entirely understood. 'My fingerprints were found on a bag? The bag that was used to suffocate Joyce?'

'Exactly! Tied around her head. But you know that, don't you?'

'No! I don't know where Joyce lives. I don't even know her. I've never met her.'

The officer places a clear plastic envelope in front of me. 'Was it because of these notes? Did she write them? Why was she sending them to you?' The policeman is following a logical path; it is difficult to argue with him because he is right.

'I don't know. I came to Ambleton this morning because I know she works on a Friday. I have never seen her before, because I have never been to Ambleton on a Friday, and I had decided that I should confront her.'

'You certainly did that!' The second police officer smirks as he joins in. 'You decided to teach Joyce a lesson that she would never forget. And you did.

'We are holding you on a charge of murder, and you will be put before a magistrate tomorrow. The custody sergeant will allow you to make one phone call.'

I don't know anyone to call.

I decide to call Desmond, as his is the only number I can think of.

He answers and I say, 'Hello Desmond. This is Mickey. I won't be able to come in tomorrow morning.'

'I know, Mickey,' he replies. Then he says, 'Why did you call me?'

'I couldn't think of anyone else.'

'Mickey, that's your problem - it's nothing to do with me.'

'I thought that you might be able to help me.'

'Help a murderer? Now why would I - why would anyone want to help you?'

'I'm not a murderer, Desmond. You know me. You know that I couldn't do anything like that.'

But isn't this what I have been promising myself to do for weeks now?

Then Desmond finishes off with, 'Donna and I are very disappointed in you. You have let us down, Mickey. I have nothing more to say to you. Please don't call us again.' And he puts the phone down.

I would have hoped for a little more support from him, but maybe he has read my mind.

What's going on? I have been arrested for a crime that I have not committed - yes, I know I was going to commit it - and I was thinking about using a Co-op bag too, but I don't think that's the point! Joyce is dead, true, but I never met her. I couldn't recognise her, but I am now accused of her murder. Desmond, Donna and I assume everybody else too, thinks that it was me.

I now understand why Sophie didn't want to speak to me.

***

Remanded in custody! I will appear before a magistrate early next week, and they expect the case to be referred to the Crown Court.

I am in a difficult situation, and my conscience is making it even more difficult for me. I have been charged with the murder I wanted to commit, but didn't. How truly 'innocent' am I? Do you believe in Karma? Is this my Karma?

I need to find a way to defend myself, and to do that I must put out of my mind all the thinking, the planning and refocus on the reality of my situation.

I didn't kill Joyce. It was somebody else, and whoever that was has set me up to take responsibility for it.

I have not discussed my plans with anyone, and I have not shown the notes to anyone either. I think that these notes are key - the police have them now, and I expect that they will return them to me at some point. They appeared in the till or in my jacket pocket, and one was sent or delivered to my house. They weren't posted, no stamp or postmark on any of them, so who did this?

I had assumed it was Joyce. Could I have been mistaken about the notes?

Maybe they were not written by her?

The most important 'evidence' against me is the Co-op bag that was used to Kill Joyce. It had my fingerprints on it. Whoever did carry out the murder would have had several opportunities to get a bag with my prints on it. I often take my shopping into ForGiving, and as the police officer found out when they came to pick me up, I have many bags at home. I need to speak to someone who can help me. I hoped that Desmond might be the one, but I was wrong there.

***

Being here is exactly like the army. It's Monday and I'm now in HMP Preston while investigations continue. I've never been inside a prison before, but the routine, the discipline - being here brings all those memories back. Being locked up in a cell is different - it was never that bad in the army, even in Helmand - and I don't like that. Even after three days, I know that I won't be able to handle prison if ever I am sentenced. I can't go outside when I want to, I can't choose when to do things - and I miss Meg terribly!

Army routine was strict, but not nearly so strict as this. And most of it seems pointless, unless the point is to break my spirit - in which case, and after only two days, it's working! And then there are the people I am locked up with - criminals! Yes, I know how obvious that is, but it is not until you are banged up with them that you realise what this means. The thought of spending years in the company of these people must be the true nature of the punishment. There is a whole social structure - over and above the official one - which is based solely on threats and violence. I've already been thumped a couple of times and spat on too - and that's in the remand wing! If I am found guilty and I have to serve a sentence, I don't think I'll cope.

Is there any light at the end of what is going to be a long and never-ending tunnel? It now appears so. I have a meeting to attend, so I am taken to a room where I find that my solicitor, Nick, is waiting for me. And he smiles.

Although I am held in connection with Joyce's murder, I have not yet been officially charged. The case must go to the Crown Prosecution Service for them to decide. Nick who seems to be on my side, says that there are many 'anomalies' with this case, and that now he is not sure that it will go to trial. He also tells me that I was on the telly last night. The police didn't mention my name, but they were keen to say that they had caught their man.

I perk up when he says this. 'Anomalies, Nick? What do you mean?'

'It's become very interesting,' Nick tells me. 'It seemed open and shut originally, and that is why you were arrested so quickly. But DI Burnham, the officer who must send the case to the CPS - told me on the phone this morning that he is not happy. He can't understand why the police went so public with things so quickly.'

'I don't get you.'

'No,' says Nick, 'Nor should you. I am not quite sure of what I am saying, or exactly what the DI meant, but the pieces don't seem to fit. The police who arrested you are trying to proceed with the case; they seem to want to see you brought to trial and convicted. But, apart from the obvious piece of evidence...'

'The Co-op bag?'

'Yes, the Co-op bag - that's all they appear to have. That's the point. DI Burnham, the new guy, says that there is not a shred of any other evidence that you were ever there, and they won't be able to front up a case for the CPS. He thinks that you were wrongly arrested, and I am asking for you to be released. That's why I am here today. I hope to get you out.'

'Fantastic! Somebody believes in me!'

Nick is not quite so positive, 'I don't know if he does believe in you. He doesn't believe the evidence - or lack of it - and that makes a difference.'

'But I didn't do it!'

'So, you say, and as your solicitor, I am representing your point of view as well as I can. We will know later today if the CPS agrees.'

I know that they can't have any other evidence because I wasn't there. The Co-op bag I assume was placed there. Then I ask - 'What other evidence have they been looking for?'

'The CCTV on the bus shows that you came into Ambleton exactly as you said. There are no traces of you being anywhere near Joyce's house, and no witnesses. You don't drive, do you?'

'No.'

'Do you have access to a car?'

'No.'

'Did someone give you a lift in on the Thursday night?'

'No - you know all this. I've answered these questions so many times over the weekend.'

'And it's these questions - and their answers that will decide what happens. If the Co-op bag is their only evidence, they can't keep you here.'

This is the first good news that I have had for a few days. 'When will they release me?'

'To be straight up about this with you, I am not sure. I hope that the CPS will get through to us today; they said they would, but I can't guarantee anything. They may decide to prosecute anyway, based on the evidence that they already have.'

'But you have just said...'

'As I said, no guarantees. There is a process in motion - it might take some stopping. I'm going to finish this interview with you now, and you will have to go back to your cell. I will get in touch with you as soon as I have any news.'

And he stands up, knocks on the door, says goodbye to me and allows a prison officer to enter and return me to my cell.

I get back, and I sit on my bench thinking about what has happened, and for the first time I begin to feel that things are moving in the right direction. Nick seems quite positive. I know the facts, and they should work on my behalf - I hope!

***

They've released me! I've been remanded on bail, but not charged. Nick was pleased with himself - he obviously did a good job.

I am not sure what my status is. I think that I am still a suspect, but as no charges have been brought, I was put in a police car and given a ride home - I thought that was kind of them.

I arrive home at about five thirty, and the first person I see is Sophie - she's returning from her walk to the Rec - and she has Meg with her.

Meg sees me and immediately pulls so hard on the leash that Sophie has to let her go, and she bounds across the road to see me. Not so, Sophie. No bounding from her! I am sure that she has no idea what to do now and frankly, neither do I.

'Hi Sophie - she's pleased to see me, isn't she? Aren't you, Meg?'

Sophie comes across the road towards me. She has her dog with her, but firmly on the leash.

'So, they let you out?' I would be struggling to think of what to say - I am struggling - but Sophie is finding it very difficult.

'I didn't do it. They had to let me go. I'm sorry if all this has embarrassed you.'

Sophie is nervous. I try to help her out. 'I'll understand if you don't want to talk to me again, but thanks for looking after Meg. She looks great.'

'She's pleased to see you - she's been pining. She keeps looking over to your place whenever time I take her out.'

'I have missed her. It's amazing how important they become, especially when you are separated from them.'

'Yes. And you are back now?'

'I am. I hope for good. It was all a mistake. I wasn't responsible for what happened, and they realised that.

So, they have let me go - even brought me home from Preston!'

'I feel awful.' She doesn't have to tell me as I can see it in her face. 'I thought you were a murderer. I am so sorry, Mickey. I've let you down.'

I bet that she doesn't feel half as awful as I do. Yes, I didn't commit the crime, so technically, I am innocent. However, as Sophie looks at me with real sorrow in her eyes, sorrow for having doubted me, I, and only I, know that I have no right to that sorrow, no right at all to have a young girl feel guilty for holding that opinion of me: an opinion that she was fully justified in holding.

Meg and I go back into the house - I look around, and apart from the disruption that the police made, it looks ok. I'll get some stuff from the shops for both Meg and for me.

Tomorrow, I will go into Ambleton - I want my job back. Let's see how Desmond responds to that!

I am Monica

Most of the people who work with me here in the shop are pleasant. They are retired, in the main. After all, it's the retired ones who have the time, and if they have a good pension and nothing much to do all day, ForGiving fills the gaps.

That describes me perfectly. Monica Bradbeer. Bill and I moved up here to our new home near Ambleton a couple of years ago, after he retired from the Council. We sold our house in Rickmansworth for what we thought was an enormous amount of money - especially when we found what we could afford here. We moved in to what we now call 'The Old Vicarage' (a white lie, the name is our invention!), and we are still amazed at how cheaply we were able to acquire it.

We were lucky, I suppose. Our Rickmansworth house was the only house we had ever owned, and we had paid off the mortgage many years ago. Bill's pension is index linked and based on his final salary so financially, we have nothing to complain about.

As soon as we arrived here, we began to fit in - at least, I tried to fit in. Bill is somewhat diffident, it is fair to say, and he doesn't go out much. He does play golf - he joined the local golf club in Winstermere, and I hardly ever see him. No change there; he played a lot of golf in Rickmansworth.

I have never had to work, never had a real job since we married. I was a secretary when Bill Bradbeer swept me off my feet. He said that he didn't want his wife to work, so I resigned from my job the week before our wedding and became a stay-at-home housewife.

It was a great sadness to both of us when we realised that we couldn't have any children. However, in compensation, I made sure that I kept busy - by 'joining in'. I was a member of so many societies and clubs, Secretary of this, Treasurer of that. When we left Rickmansworth, I think that I probably left a gaping hole in the social fabric of the town.

Of course, I would have liked to have had a family, or at least to have had one child. We lived in a lovely home and with my not working, I would have had plenty of time to be a good mum. There is still a void there, and I do feel it. I remember that I even broached the idea of adoption with Bill when it became apparent that we would never become parents. He was quite angry at the thought - adamant that he would not have 'a stranger's child in our house', so after a time, I accepted that I would never become a mother.

It hasn't stopped us having a successful marriage; all in all, we have been happy. Instead of children, we focused our attention on other things: we created our beautiful home and we filled it with stylish and tasteful furnishings, decorative items and such like. We began to specialise in oriental objects, and I think that we have become quite expert as some of the purchases that we have made have certainly appreciated in value.

So, we've our small collections of various kinds to keep us busy. Antiques are our 'thing', and as well as that, I have always had my clubs and societies.

We have always been able to travel extensively, seeing ourselves more as travellers rather than tourists. We don't 'do' beach holidays: it is the history and the traditions of the places that we visit that is of interest - Bill is quite adamant about this. And although I have often been tempted by the idea of lounging about on a beach, Bill has convinced me that we must learn as much as possible about everywhere we visit, so that we can talk knowledgeably about our travels in social situations.

And that's another thing we have in common with Desmond, apparently. He is a traveller too - and a collector! Oh, Desmond! He is the manager of the ForGiving shop where I work - and he seems to be a knowledgeable man. He and I seem to have hit it off, and he has said that when his wife next returns from France, we might meet for a bite of supper. I would be quite interested to see his collections, so Bill and I might think about accepting their invitation.

I want to say that working at ForGiving has proved to be the most interesting diversion that I have found since we arrived up here. For some reason, I never thought of working in a charity shop back home. I preferred clubs and societies where there was a strong social side. And of course, Bill had his Masons and the golf club, and I am sure that you know how busy a social calendar that calls for.

Bill transferred to the Masonic Lodge up here as soon as we arrived; the least said about that the better. He went to two or three meetings and then decided to stop. He hasn't told me why exactly, but I think I can guess. The members of the Rickmansworth Lodge were drawn from, how shall I say it - from a higher social stratum? I think that it would be fair to say that. We did attend one of their Ladies' nights. I can't say that I enjoyed it, and I certainly will not be returning for a second time. It was not quite what we were expecting.

Yes, I have to be more accepting, less judgemental - I know. Things are different now that we live in the 'North'.   They are a little less refined up here - kinder, more neighbourly, but they definitely prefer simpler pleasures.

A little snippet to give you an idea: Bill and I never rode to hounds, but we did enjoy the Hunt as it went about its business. There is something curiously attractive about the Hunting Red jackets and it's exciting to watch the riders leaping over (and sometimes failing to leap over) ditches and fences.

The local Hunt here goes out on a Thursday, so we decided to have a look. It was a great disappointment - no horses! They walk with their hounds! No spectacle at all, just one slightly seedy looking man in a red jacket, so we gave up on that straightaway.

However, on the positive side, working in ForGiving turns out to be a revelation. Most of the ladies who volunteer seem to be cut from the same kind of cloth as me. They have migrated here from other, more sophisticated backgrounds to throw themselves into the hurly burly of a more Northern lifestyle.

Because there are so many of us - we all seem to be members of the same clubs now; we are all on the same committees, there is a sense of being able to 'insulate' ourselves from the harsher realities of living here. There are a few local ladies who also work in the shop, but they seem content to get on with things. They happily get involved and don't seem to 'want' anything out of working for ForGiving. It's the whole idea of doing something worthwhile that appeals, and they fold the clothes, man the tills, make the teas and coffees and seem genuinely happy.

My introduction to 'retail' here in the ForGiving shop was an eye opener, I can tell you. Having to deal with the general public in ways that I had never been required to do before opened my eyes somewhat.

I have got the hang of it now, but it was touch and go for a while - I think it's fair to say. The other ladies who work in the shop were understanding, and after three or four sessions in the back, where I folded clothes and ironed things, I was asked if I would like to work on the till - in the shop itself.

The till is electronic, and it is supposed to make life easier for us. What I have noticed, however, is that almost every evening, no matter who has been on the till, it takes up to an hour to complete the accounts for the day. This is frustrating for everyone concerned, but we get on with it. I am sure that there is an easier way, but we are volunteers, and it is not as if anyone is paying us overtime, so we stay in the shop until the till is resolved, or until Desmond takes over and asks us to go home.

Dinner, on those evenings when I work in ForGiving, is what you would call a 'moveable feast', and Bill is becoming increasingly annoyed, as he often cooks the meal, and then sometimes sees it incinerate in front of him. I've tried telling him to wait until I get home, but at our time of life, it is always better that we eat earlier, isn't it? And Bill is firmly of that opinion.

The till might be one challenge that I have about mastered, but the customers provide many more, now that I deal with them on a regular basis.

Last week, a woman came into the shop and selected about five different dresses and skirts. She asked if she could try them on, and I said yes. When she returned, she only had one skirt to give me. I asked her, politely, where the other items were, and she said she had left them in the changing room. She then said thank you and goodbye.

She hadn't left them in the changing room at all! She'd gone out of the shop wearing them! What are you to do in circumstances like that? Was I at fault? Can you contemplate anybody stealing from a charity shop? No, I can't either.

I looked outside into the street to see which way she had gone, but she was nowhere to be seen. I phoned Desmond to seek his advice. He seemed quite short when he answered the phone and told me that he wasn't working that day. I think that I had expected a little more in the way of understanding from him. He asked me to write it down in the daybook - the notebook that we use for day-to-day messages.

I think that he must be a very busy man because apart from managing this shop, he has many other commitments, both to ForGiving and elsewhere. I believe that he does some work for some international organisations. I hope to be able to ask him about that as it sounds quite exciting.

I am a little more prepared for strange customers now, and I watch out for anyone who takes clothes into the changing room. I only allow them to take two items - I made sure that I put that in the daybook too as a suggestion, but I don't know if it has been taken on board by anyone else.

Although he seems to lack empathy sometimes, I think that Desmond, our manager, must have realised that I have skills that make me a cut above the ordinary. As I said, Bill and I have always collected things, Netsuke - always in ivory, was one of our specialities, and when I mentioned this to Desmond, he seemed to be quite impressed.

If you know a lot about some aspect of collecting, as we do with regard to Netsuke, I guess you have an eye, and it is the eye that matters.

People bring things into the shop all the time, and sometimes quite valuable items are mixed in with things that we mostly throw away. You need to have someone who can distinguish between the two, as it were, and Desmond has seen that quality, 'discernment', in me.

He tells me that he and his wife are also collectors. They have a little house on an estate on the outskirts of the village; not far from where we live, in fact. They keep some of their collection at their house, but it is too small for them to be able to keep everything there. Luckily, they have another house, in France. Desmond says that it is a chateau, a small one - so grand! He was telling someone in the shop today that his wife is there now; she is an interior designer, so that must be a handy talent to have in the family.

Anyway, the valuation of items requiring an informed opinion becomes another string to my bow. It is me who is asked to decide if an object is valuable enough to be displayed in one of our lockable glass cases. Quite an important task, and I take some pride in doing it as professionally as I can.

More often than not, I find myself coming into the shop two or three mornings a week. And as I have said, most of the ladies I work with are pleasant. I think that they now see me as the antiques 'expert', so items are put aside 'for Monica's attention'.

Our move to the Lakes has worked quite well for me, and I would be more comfortable about it if I was able to say the same for Bill. To be quite honest with you, I don't think that I can say that for Bill. He is not happy; he is becoming more and more - isolated is the word, yes, isolated.

Everyone I come in to contact with, particularly at ForGiving, is pleasant - even the people who I would prefer not to socialise with have qualities that are attractive. We are all of a similar age, and no matter from where we originate, we seem to hold the same kind of values. And that is comforting, isn't it?

I am not sure if I should tell you this, but there are two people whom I simply cannot like, try as I might. I can't forge a relationship with the man called Mickey - the name alone stops me in my tracks. I like the name 'Michael', and I could probably put up with 'Mike', but the word 'Mickey' doesn't want to come out of my throat.

I simply can't say a name like that. And his name is not the only one - I hate some modern-day girls' names too and would find it impossible to strike up a relationship with someone called 'Tenisa' or 'Vegas'. But this man Mickey adds to the effect that his name has on me with his quite disgusting physical presence. He looks like a down and out - straggly shoulder length hair, often in a ponytail - in my opinion, always a mistake in an older man. And, if you were to get close to him - which I never do, you might find that he smells a little ripe too!

The other person I am finding difficulty with is 'Sally'. But for other reasons - I mean that the reasons that I cannot speak to her are different from the obstacles between Mickey and me. The main obstacle is that I am not sure that she is a 'she' at all! I am sure that she is a man who is dressed as a woman, and I daren't ask! I simply smile and ignore her, saying hello on occasion, but not much more. She is polite, always says hello to me, and the other ladies in the shop all seem to like her.

I have heard of these people - never met one, of course, and even if she did tell me that she was a man dressed as a woman, what would I do with that information? I have no experience of dealing with this kind of thing at all, so I ignore the issue completely.

That apart, coming here to work is something that I now look forward to, especially as Bill has now started to play more golf than ever he did before.

Sometimes I don't see him for days on end. We have slept in separate rooms for many years, so often I don't hear him come in. If he is going to be away for a night or two, he always lets me know. That seems to be happening a little more often, maybe three or four times a month: it does seem that he is playing a lot of golf!

***

Bill has not been playing golf! In my mind are all sorts of words that I would never dream of saying! What do I do with them - those words?

We left Rickmansworth over two years ago, at least I did, and I had assumed that Bill had too. But no, those nights he spends away have not been with his golfing buddies: he has been spending them in Rickmansworth.

I found this out when an old friend emailed me. She said that she had seen Bill and wondered if I was available one day to have lunch with her, like we did in the old days.

She assumed that I was with him in Rickmansworth, and I had to work hard to maintain any dignity at all while I replied. I was able to say that no, I wasn't with Bill this time, as I had an engagement that I had to honour here in Ambleton. A white lie, but a lie nonetheless.

In all our years together, I felt that I never had any reason to doubt him.

What had he been doing? Of course, I tackled him as soon as he got home - all guns blazing. 'Alison called me. Said that you were in Rickmansworth. Why were you there? Who were you with, Bill?'

He looked astonished; couldn't think of how to respond. The logical side of his brain must have been telling him that whenever he went to Rickmansworth, the chances of somebody seeing him were quite high. After all, he has lived there for most of his life. At that same moment, the other side of his brain was trying to dream up some creative excuse, but nothing was happening. He shouldn't have been surprised at his lack of creativity. I wasn't - I had lived with him for a long time.

Eventually, he tells me. There was bluster to begin with, but when I have my dander up - which is not too often, thankfully - I can be pretty formidable, I can tell you.

He's been conducting an affair with his old secretary, Rowena - wait for it - for over six years! The move to the Lakes was, he says, a good idea, because it was meant to force him to break it off. But he tells me that he has tried, and he can't - break it off, that is. (He should have asked me. I would have broken it off for him!)

He loves Rowena, and he goes back to Rickmansworth to see her. And what's more, he wants to return to Rickmansworth as soon as he can - so that he can live with her. This will involve her leaving her husband too - so it's a right mess, if you ask me, which, of course, he hasn't!

I read all kinds of novels, and in them most husbands who cheat on their wives are portrayed as conniving, lying s****, forgive my French. Conducting a six-year affair is the province of a conniving, lying s***, I grant you, but this part of the affair, the denouement - and the obsessive need to lie about it after being found out - is not there at all, not in Bill. He seems relieved.

I don't have to drag it out of him - it flows! I can see that it is a great release - something that has been pent up in him for a long time.

There I go again! Too much empathy, that's my trouble. That and 'selective blindness', I guess. Did I not see? Were there no signals? Am I completely stupid? Yes, yes and no to those questions. Particularly the last. I am not stupid: I have been deceived.

I grant that another woman in my situation might have been more perceptive and picked up more in the way of signals. I should have questioned his more and more frequent 'golf' trips, but in my defence, we had settled into an amenable relationship where we lived in the same space, but our lives had for some time been lived in parallel rather than together as one.

I thought that I would be angrier than I am now. Maybe a few years ago? Hormones? That's it! Other priorities now. Whatever he has in his mind - and I am sure that there is something cooking away there - I will make sure that it's not going to involve my losing either my house or the benefits of the pension that I have helped him so assiduously to build up.

I will make things difficult for him, and that is as much as I am prepared to say for now. This matter needs thinking about, and although Bill, I am sure, wants to make things happen quickly so that he can be off and away with his 'doxie' - lovely word, that - never thought I'd use it, he can spin in the wind for as long as it takes me to work out my strategy.

***

Bill has left me, and I think that he has gone back to Rickmansworth. He said he will arrange to have his things picked up when everything is more settled. He will have a long wait!

He did have some difficulty finding suitable clothes to wear, as I had had the time to cut off the legs of most of his trousers, and I was able to lay waste to his shirts and suits with a handy can of paint.

The golfing stuff which frankly, I never liked anyway, simply had to be cut up because, in my opinion, pouring a can of paint over those ludicrously loud trousers and the Pringle jumpers would only improve them.

I found it quite difficult to destroy his golf clubs, but by putting the handle in between the bars of our front gate, and pushing and pulling very hard, I managed to bend most of them into some quite dramatic shapes. I feel justified in this trivial act of passive aggression; it's a rite of passage in these circumstances, isn't it? So, don't begrudge me that small pleasure - thank you!

We've always had two cars, so I will be able to get around without any inconvenience at all. I will continue my work at ForGiving: Bill always kept away from my charitable activities, so I doubt that most of the people I work with even know of him.

Yes, there are matters that will challenge me soon, and I am fully aware of this. At some point, I must obtain some legal advice as to how I should proceed.

But he first decision, and I have already made it, is a simple one: Bill doesn't come back. I am not sure that he will want to - this is not hubris on my part - I simply know that I don't love him enough to want to have him back. So, if it all backfires on him and Rowena turns out to have been his mid-life crisis: tough! The truth is that part of me is quite pleased that he's gone.

The more practical matters - the house, an income for me - will have to be discussed quite soon. But as I told you before, we own our property outright, it is in joint names, and we have no debt.

***

I received a letter from Bill's solicitor - he was the solicitor for both of us, but the tone of the letter suggests that he is no longer on my side. Golf buddies!

Bill wants us to sell the house and split the proceeds. No mention is made of my receiving any other payment - nothing is mentioned about his pension, or about the savings account that we have.

I immediately go online. Our savings account is in joint names, and the balance is still there! Even I know what to do now, and I do it.

I transfer the whole of the balance into a separate savings account that I have in my name. I have kept that account for years, rarely have I used it, and then only for minor transactions. But it is a useful port of call for an entirely new purpose.

The transfer is made immediately. I don't know if it can be blocked or recalled, but I am happy to wait and see what happens. Even if somehow the transaction is stopped, it will be a signal to Bill that I am determined to make things difficult for him. Sell the house? He can spin on that thought! Sorry about the vulgarity, but that's how I feel.

I told you that when we sold our house in Rickmansworth, I was amazed at how much money we made. We were able to buy our house here in the Lakes, and we still had over three hundred thousand pounds spare! That is the money that I hope that I have transferred to my own account. It may well not happen; I am realistic enough to know that Bill or his solicitors might be able to put a block on it, but if nothing else, a signal will have been sent. Yes, that is what this is about - I have sent a signal!

You remember that man Mickey that I told you about? I knew there was something strange about him. It is big news here: he has been charged with murder - the murder of one of the ladies who worked here in the shop! It could have been me!

Joyce, an elderly lady who usually works here on a Friday was murdered in her home! She was suffocated by having a plastic bag put over her head. The TV news said that fingerprints found on the bag led them to the flat of another of the ForGiving volunteers - Mickey!

It was all over the newspapers. The TV came to the ForGiving shop, interviewing volunteers. Our manager, Desmond, gave a short speech and said on behalf of the 'ForGiving community' that our 'thoughts and prayers were with Joyce's family at this time'. He likes the spotlight, I have noticed.

I have told you that I couldn't relate to that man, Mickey, but that is a long stretch away from my ever thinking that he was capable of killing anyone. When I heard about it, I was surprised at my reaction. I immediately thought no, it wasn't him. And leaving fingerprints? Wouldn't you wear gloves? I mean, everybody watches the TV. One of the hidden benefits of wall-to-wall police dramas is that we all know what to do in the event of our having to murder someone.

The police have interviewed all the volunteers, including me. I explained - when asked by a pleasant police detective - why I did not think that Mickey was the murderer.

This detective seemed interested in my theory - especially about the fingerprints: I said that to leave them on the plastic bag - it was a Co-op bag - was simply an act of stupidity. Apparently, that thought was in his mind too. But Mickey is to be charged, and the police have much more experience than I have, and of course, they have the evidence. I only have this feeling in my tummy to go on, but it is a strong feeling, very strong.

Oh, and that transfer of funds to my own account was blocked! Bastards! - Sorry, my French again!

I went to see a solicitor here in Ambleton and I have asked her to act for me. She was so friendly and understanding that I was immediately convinced that I want her on my side. She tells me that there is every chance that I can come out of this well; 'smelling of roses' was the term she used.

I try to make another attempt at accessing our joint account - but for a smaller sum this time. And it works! I transfer twenty thousand, and it is not blocked or recalled.

And I am now thinking about getting a job. After all these years, I will have to fend for myself. I am only fifty-three now and can't expect a pension for a long time yet. I may well have to give up the ForGiving job, as it is only voluntary work. But I do like it, and I have noticed that I am quite good at it. There are vacancies in shops, hotels and cafes here, so I am hopeful, but not super-confident as I am getting on a bit. However, because this is a tourist town - and, because many of the eastern Europeans who have kept the local economy going are returning to their own countries, thanks to Brexit, I may well be lucky.

***

Isn't it strange how things happen as if they are meant to be? Out of the blue, after an interesting conversation about the provenance of a couple of paintings that came into the shop, Desmond mentioned that he is thinking of resigning his position as manager of ForGiving.

My first thought is along the lines of Oh no! Another person leaving, along with Joyce and that Mickey - leaving for altogether different reasons, of course. And I know that Donna will not stay on if Desmond leaves, as they live their lives in each other's pockets more than any couple I have ever met.

But my rather selfish thoughts in the staffing rota direction end abruptly when Desmond suggests that I think about applying for his position - the job of manager at ForGiving! He says that I have shown myself to be a 'natural manager' - his words - and that with my expertise in the collections arena, I would be an ideal choice.

Now this happy coincidence has occurred before anyone knows of the issues that I have with Bill, with my marriage and with what I thought might be a desperate need to get myself a job. I appear to have a job being offered to me.

I thank Desmond and say that I am flattered that he has such faith in me. He says it would be his choice to have someone like me take over from him, as we understand each other, we are 'sympatico'. And he looks at me and smiles - slightly strangely, I must say.

The demands of his house in France and the additional international work that he has been asked to do, all hush hush, apparently, means that he has not the time to devote to the work of ForGiving that he feels is necessary. He doesn't like the thought of letting people down, and I understand that. He adds that it is his belief that you must be prepared to give one hundred percent when you are in a position of authority.

While I do agree with the sentiment, that is not exactly how most people believe that Desmond sees things. He does take a lot of time off - so many holidays - and he does seem to have delegated many of his responsibilities - such as the rotas - to volunteers like Julia and me. However, putting all that to one side, if he were to put in a good word for me, that could only help, couldn't it?

And I think that I will go for it! It could be an answer to my immediate difficulty, and I do enjoy the work. I would probably have to go on some training courses, and that's no bad thing. I am not too familiar with spreadsheets and so on, but a computer doesn't frighten me as I have been using email for years. Yes, this seems like a plan - I will follow it up!

***

The battle has started, and Bill is asking me to agree to selling our home. I have taken legal advice too, and I have decided to say no.

He owns half of the house, no argument there, but it is he who moved out, he who left me.

Lisa, my solicitor, has suggested that if I don't want to move out, and I don't, we try to do something about it. She believes that we can get the court to grant me something called a 'Martin' order. I had never heard of it before, but it could postpone my having to leave our family home.

If we divorce - and that will happen soon, I can tell you now - the judge could give me permission to continue living in my home - even though Bill and I will have been divorced. The home would be sold, and the assets divided, but only after I chose to leave, or for example, if I were to marry again - or when either Bill or I die. I don't know much about this kind of arrangement, but Lisa says that it could be exactly the solution for me.

I like this idea, not least because it will put a spanner in someone's works, ha ha! I like it also because I don't see why I should have to leave my house and a lifestyle that I have come to enjoy because Bill decided to cheat on me. Lisa seems to be on my side too.

Alternatively, Bill could let me have my half of the value of the house, and half the savings in our joint bank account. And then there is the pension. If we divorce, I will become entitled to a proportion of his pension. Lisa tells me that there are several ways in which a settlement could be reached, but all in all, she is confident that I will come out of this rather well.

I have just noticed that I have written 'Bill could let me have...' Ha! I am starting to feel that I have almost come out of a hypnotic trance, a trance in which Bill, my master, 'allows' or 'doesn't allow' me to follow a certain course of action.

That stops as of now. As if Bill Bradbeer 'allowing' me to do anything is to apply anymore! I am living in the house - 'possession is nine points' - well you know the rest, and I am going nowhere. I have had my solicitor arrange that all transfers and withdrawals from our joint bank account need both of our signatures, and she has also established that I have a legal right to a proportion of the pension that Bill is entitled to from his work. (I created the household from which he could function over all those years, and my rights in this situation are well defined.)

No permissions needed! It is Bill who is going to have to come to me to be 'allowed' to take any next step. This is something that I won't forget - and frankly, I don't think Lisa will allow me to forget - she is a bit of a feminist, I think. All good stuff!

***

That man Mickey was held in custody over the weekend and released on the Monday. He is now on bail. The police seemed sure that it was he who killed Joyce. I have checked all this out because beavering away at the back of my mind is that Co-op bag. I am certain that nobody, not even the world's most stupid person, would leave their fingerprints on a murder weapon such as that. Why did he not take it away with him? The whole affair is niggling me. And it's not as if I care! It wouldn't matter if I never saw the man again, but there is something wrong with all this, and I am wondering what I could do to help Mickey.

I'm not entirely sure of the timeline, but as I understand it, Joyce was killed overnight on the Thursday. Mickey went back to Winstermere on the Friday - after working a morning shift in Ambleton. There he was met by the police, and they arrested him. They then went to his room and they removed some notes that had been sent to him, and which were apparently written by Joyce.

Maybe he did do it and I am fantasising. The evidence seems to suggest that he is guilty, but why is my stomach telling me otherwise?

***

I am soon to be the new ForGiving manager! Three days a week, three weeks holiday a year. Not bad for someone who hasn't worked since she was in her early twenties.

Desmond came to congratulate me. He said that he had put in a good word for me - he had interviewed me along with Patsy, the regional manager who now becomes my boss.

He also invited me to meet him at his home. He said that Donna was away in France and now might be a good time for us to get to know each other a little better, and would I like to come over one evening for a bite to eat?

I was able to kick that suggestion into the long grass with a smile and a maybe, so that I could focus on the new responsibilities that I have. At first glance, my role doesn't seem to be too complicated. Patsy told me that the main difficulty is remembering that my staff are not employees, but volunteers. Tell me about it! That was my reaction, but of course, I did not say it out loud.

Desmond has always been polite - maybe a little deferential - to me, but he does seem to annoy some of the volunteers. Truth is that some of them have stopped making themselves available, and now with Joyce and Mickey out of the equation too, we have a staffing problem already.

And I was right about Donna. She will not be coming in again now that Desmond is leaving. She must have returned from France, as Desmond announced the change of regime by writing a florid note in the book. D&D are moving on to 'new opportunities' that have presented themselves.

With my new-found sense of independence, the 'liberated woman' in me is slightly concerned for Donna. She simply won't do anything on her own, but always does exactly what Desmond says. That is bad enough, in my newly-developed sense of what women should be thinking about, but it is her brittleness that particularly worries me.

What I mean is that she lives in his shadow, and gets her strength from there, not from herself. She can be extremely bossy - I told you that she has written notices all over the place, seeing herself as joint manager, and telling people how they should behave. It is this that has put so many of the volunteers off.

One of them challenged her, most politely, I thought. In essence, she said that she had no idea of how to speak to people. Donna has ignored that woman ever since - cutting her dead when they meet in the shop.

When they do leave, I don't think that D&D will be missed too much.

And I was right about having to go on a course! I don't start work officially for three weeks, but before then I have been asked to go for an induction where I will learn about the charity's reporting systems, how to manage the computer, and how to reconcile the till at the end of the day. One of my first acts will be to make sure that the cash reconciliation is speeded up - Desmond often takes more than an hour to cash up.

Some time ago, he decided to take over that responsibility for himself. I feel that was the wrong thing to do as it means that he is responsible for all cashing up. That's not good enough, and I will want to do something to fix that. It will be a priority for me, as I have no intention of spending all of my evenings counting money! One of my first initiatives must be a training course to get the volunteers to cash up at the end of their shift.

The news has got around that D&D are leaving. Two ladies told me today that they would like to come back when I have taken over. I was pleased to hear that. Maybe our staffing problems won't be as great as I had feared.

You remember that Desmond had invited Bill and me around for a meal when I first came to work at ForGiving.   He felt that we had some interests in common? Well, today he said that he thought such an idea was 'inappropriate', now that Bill and I were separated. He made no mention of the other, more intimate invitation that was for me only to accept.

I did not know what to think of the two quite separate messages, but I concluded that frankly D&D are a bit up themselves. They seem to have an idealised version of what a life should be, and marriages splitting up don't seem to fit into that kind of vision. It's probably close to the worldview that I held up until recently, so I should not hold that against them too much. In any event, the more I have seen of them and their ludicrous posturing, the less I have wanted to see them on a social level. And there is something more than simple hypocrisy in Desmond's suggestiveness.

I am not sure that he tells the truth most of the time. I'm not saying that he is a liar, but I have noticed that he does embellish things. During just one afternoon last week, while talking on the phone or chatting with customers, he referred to himself as 'Dr' Blain, told another person that he had studied at Oxford, and a third that he had played cricket at 'county level'.

I don't believe him: I don't think all that can be true, because he told me on another occasion that he was a trained artist, but that he also had a degree in archaeology. If you add to that his work for this secret international organisation - yet other people have told me that until he retired he was a laboratory technician in a school - I wonder what makes him need to say these things?

He tells me that when he leaves, he is going to be retained as the 'valuables expert', the person who prices what we think are the more valuable items that come into the shop, and he looks forward to working with me in a 'different kind of relationship' - his words.

I have a surprise for him. As I have already been in that role for some time, appointed to it when I was more favourable in his eyes, I don't feel that we will have the need of his services. I will ask someone like Julia to work with me on this, and I think that we will make a success of the enterprise.

Oh, you know that little man, Mickey - the one that I was talking about? He was released, and all charges have been dropped. I don't quite know why, but it seems that the evidence against him wasn't as strong as the police had thought. It wasn't him who killed Joyce, and the chief constable had to go on television and say that their 'enquiries were following a different route', and a new arrest was likely soon.

I knew it wasn't Mickey: he's too ineffectual to do something like that. I am sure that the process of murdering somebody - planning it and carrying it out - would take much more of an effort than he could muster. I think we all would like to know who the real murderer is. Releasing Mickey obviously suggests that a killer is still walking around somewhere, and the sooner they catch him, the more peacefully we will be sleeping in our beds.

***

It's been a busy few days and I have lots to report! Isn't it exciting how life takes strange turns? Before I took on my job at ForGiving, Bill was about to leave me, and I was contemplating a stressful, lonely late middle age.

Lisa, my young feminist solicitor - she laughed when I called her that - has been simply brilliant. As I write this (I am metaphorically crossing my fingers, of course), Bill and I have been able to agree to an amicable divorce settlement. I say amicable, but frankly I can't see how Bill can see it that way - maybe he really is loved up.

I will remain here in my house and can live in it as long as I wish. If I choose to leave, I will be required to sell up, and the proceeds of the sale of the house will then be split between the two of us. That's the 'Martin' agreement for you!

Half of our joint savings and half of Bill's pension - this is what I had hoped for, but never expected - is kicking in about now, and because I know I can remain settled here in the Lake District, I am feeling much more confident about my future.

The job is great! It doesn't pay much, but I don't have any great expenses to worry about. I can live well, drive my little car and still have something left over without dipping into my savings. Feeling settled like this allows me to sleep comfortably in my bed at night.

And talking about sleeping in my bed - should I let you know that I now have a companion in mine? First time in a long time, and I didn't have to go to a Greek island to find him like that lady in the film. I had thought of keeping this a secret, but then I thought what the hell!

A few weeks ago, because I needed some work doing to fix some roof slates that had come off during a storm, one of the ladies at ForGiving gave me the number of a man who, she said, 'is able to fix everything'.

This man came to my house a few days later to do the work. He is Polish, and his name is Voytek. Long story short: yes, he's at least fifteen years younger than I am, but from the moment we met and before he did any work for me, I knew that he was perfect - not just as an odd job man - but as a lover!

He is kind, he makes me laugh, and he is wonderful in bed - in my bed! I am blushing now; I never believed that I would hear myself even thinking those thoughts, never mind mentioning them to someone else - but it is true.

And, before you say anything: I know! Older woman, younger man. 'Yada yada yada' as he would say. Voytek is independent. He lives in his own flat in Bowness on Winstermere, not far from here, and he is not after me for my money - as he knows nothing about my financial situation.

We go 'Dutch' on everything that we buy or spend.   Sometimes he stays over, often he doesn't. And let me tell you something else. Even if he has other lovers, even if he has a hundred other lovers, that doesn't matter to me one little bit. When he is with me he treats me as if I were the only woman in the world.

I find myself saying this through gritted teeth because in the so called 'conventional' relationship, the marriage and so on that I had with Bill over all those years, I never felt like I feel now - not once, not ever.

Thanks Bill! You didn't mean to, but you have made me happy. I am sensible enough - 'mature enough' might be a better way of saying it - to realise that this might not go on forever, but while I have Voytek, I am making up for lost time - and loving every moment of it.

And those wagging ForGiving tongues that worried me so much when Bill and I split? They have been talking, I know that, but when those women look at me, they look at me in a different kind of way. I can tell what they are thinking, and I can also see those green eyes shining at me - and I rather like that too.

Desmond has sent me an email asking when we should meet up. I replied, thanking him for his interest, but informing him that we had been able to make other plans relating to our valuations, and that we would not be troubling him. He has not got back to me.

***

Today Mickey came into the shop. My second managerial dilemma! First D&D and now Mickey. He was surprised that Desmond and Donna were going to be leaving, and even more surprised that I was to take over as manager.

Although I know quite a lot about Mickey - most of it gossip, of course, this was the first time that I actually had to speak to him. And it wasn't something I could avoid, now that I am the manager here.

He came in expecting to see Desmond, but when he knew it was me he had to speak to, he asked if we could go into my office as he had something to ask of me. My office is the pokiest little space you can imagine - impossible for us to have any conversation at all without others listening to us.

I think that I surprised myself when I suggested to Mickey that we go out for a coffee - for our confidential chat. He agreed, although I could see that he too was surprised. But this is the new me! I am making decisions - and choosing options that were inconceivable such a short time ago.

We popped into the 'Copper Kettle', a little artisan cafe a few doors down the street, and I found myself quite at ease as I sat down with this funny little man. Yes, he looks strange, a little weird - with his straggly ponytail and sad face, but a previous version of Monica would never have deigned to acknowledge him, never mind sit down with him for a chat.

Simply put, now that he is back at ForGiving, he wondered if I might be able to give him a little more responsibility. Nothing fancy, but after his recent experiences with the police, he said that he wanted to get down to some real work for a change. He was hoping that there might be a manager's job in another of the ForGiving shops - although he would prefer to keep on working here.

And then he asked what I thought was a particularly clever question - he said that now we all knew that he was innocent of all charges, he wondered if he could become my assistant.

'Innocent'. That's the first time I have heard anyone use that term referring to Mickey, and frankly, I was pleased to hear it, even though it was he who used the term, and I would have perhaps felt more comfortable had I also heard it from the lips of a police officer.

But it was the 'assistant' thing that fired my imagination. I went one stage further! I decided - entirely without discussing this with anyone - to make my second executive decision. I have decided to employ Mickey myself. That is, I said that yes, he could have a role as my assistant, and I would be happy to pay him a small wage. This would be a private arrangement, and a condition of it is that he does not discuss it with anyone.

My reasoning was that this man obviously needs a leg up, and I am now in a position to help him, what with my having more money than I know what to do with it. If I pay him a wage, if I employ him, he will be able to think better of himself, and maybe get into a mindset where he might go for a proper job. It's always easier to get a job from a job, rather than from unemployment because you can feel so much more confident being able to say that yes, you are currently employed.

Of course, I'm not sure how this is going to work out - it was entirely spontaneous - and I am sure that there will be all kinds of tax and benefits issues, but I made that decision. Me! And both Mickey and I seem to be entirely comfortable with it. In fact, I think that there were a few tears as Mickey said goodbye and went to catch his bus.

It is said that actors can have a sort of 'out of body' experience when they are performing. They can see themselves, watch themselves at work, so that they are in the right position on the stage, aware of the lighting and the entrances of their colleagues. They can make small adjustments to their performance styles to meet the needs of the stage or the TV camera, and they can observe themselves in action, as it were - watching their own performances.

At that moment, I dearly wished that I could have seen myself in conversation with Mickey that afternoon. I would have been able to observe myself acting like a professional manager. Then I would have seen myself finishing the day and making my way home to my lovely house ready to share a glass of wine - and maybe something more - with Voytek.

Julia and Gordon

Working at the ForGiving shop in Ambleton is the fourth charity shop job that I have had, and up until recently, it has been the most satisfying. I started working here about six years ago, and as the years have progressed, I have found myself taking on more and more responsibilities.

Consequently, I was happy to let my other minor obligations go, and often ForGiving takes up most of my week. I usually work four half days each week, and sometimes, if there is an unexpected absentee or a mistake on the rota, I am the first person to be called in to bridge the gap.

That mistake on the rota strikes home to me because if it ever happens - and sometimes it does - it is now entirely my fault, as I am responsible for drawing it up each week.

I have a challenge to meet now as I must find a replacement for Jo, one of our volunteers. Desmond, the manager, told me that she won't be available on Tuesday and Thursday for a while, and this minutes after Monica phoned to say that something had come up, and she too would be unavailable on Thursday. She has some personal matters to attend to, I was told, although Desmond would not divulge.

Solving this issue ought to fall at Desmond's door - it being his job, but as he has devolved responsibility for the rota to me, I can't expect much assistance from that quarter.

If there is a cloud on the horizon, and frankly, I can see it looming, it is whether I am going to be able to maintain my sense of equilibrium in my relationship with Desmond - and with his pushy wife, Donna.

Desmond has been manager for about three years, and from being a friendly and helpful colleague, Desmond and his wife, Donna, have morphed into a monstrous kind of double act. They behave as one - in everything! Desmond's opinions are those of Donna. When she has an opinion, and now she seems to be having more and more of them, that opinion is always underwritten by Desmond, in every particular.

This has been of some consequence to me, and it is something, along with several other challenges, that I must come to terms with.

The upshot is that Donna has become a *de-facto* manager! Soon after Desmond was appointed into the role, Donna began to appear with him and she quickly assumed that she was entitled to use his authority to achieve her own ForGiving - related objectives.

She 'reorganised' the room at the back of the shop where we sort the clothing as it comes in, and to be fair to her, she did a pretty good job.

But it was her manner, and especially the way she then went on to appropriate the window displays that was so infuriating. I don't think that I am the only person who objects to her high-handedness; many of the ladies who had been working at ForGiving for a long time also were miffed, I could tell.

Suddenly, there were notices everywhere! 'Do This!', 'Don't do that!', 'Ask permission from Donna before you do this again!' I must tell you that ladies of a certain age don't take too kindly to being told what to do in such a peremptory fashion. We are volunteers, after all.

The upshot of this was that a few of the ladies stopped putting their names down, and those who remain are much less willing to go the extra mile; to help out when situations such as the absences on the rota for next week crop up. Bottom line - more work and more stress for me.

I am particularly careful not to take my stress home. At the end of any ForGiving day, and if I have been stressed, it's sad to have to recount that my husband is likely to be much less supportive than he used to be. It's understandable; he had a run-in with Desmond some time ago so, if I were to mention that Desmond has let me down again in any way, his 'one size fits all' response is to say, 'And what did you expect from that dickhead?' or some such unpleasant rejoinder.

And the real reason for his lack of support? Early retirement - and I am putting it down to that. He will be leaving at the end of the summer term, not because he wishes to retire, but because he has been asked to retire. I am sure that's why he has become so prickly recently, and why I am careful not to make him even more so, if I can help it.

My husband, Gordon, is head teacher in a residential school for children with behavioural problems. It's near Churchfield, and as we live near Kendal, he and I travel in opposite directions when we go off to work. There's a metaphor there!

Gordon often mentions that when he first started in special education, the children who came to his kind of school were mainly naughty boys. Over the years that seems to have changed, in that the children he now must work with are not simply naughty, some of them seem to be downright evil too. Many of them, particularly those who have been physically or sexually abused, are almost impossible to handle, and teaching them anything often plays second fiddle to keeping them from killing each other.

And, in Gordon's school, they have started accepting girls! The theory is that the addition of female pupils will help create a more family-like atmosphere. Evidently, it does nothing of the sort. The pupils now seem to spend most of their time trying to get into each other's bedrooms, so if it is a family atmosphere that is being created, it is one with a lot of incest in the mix!

Most of Gordon's time is spent employing staff - the turnover of staff members is frightening. Male teachers, particularly, come to find themselves being challenged every moment of the day. The kids wind them up mercilessly, deliberately trying to provoke them into angry responses. At that point, the more sensible ones realise that if they stay, sometime soon they are going to be provoked so much that they will lash out, either to defend themselves from attack, or because their sense of self-esteem demands it of them.

Those who stay are those who can realise that these children have been let down so much in their young lives that they need to test all their relationships to destruction. Those teachers, says Gordon, are the people of real value; some of them are wonderfully professional. Gordon is - or was - one of those. The others who stay are those who Gordon refers to as 'the walking dead' - men and women who have completely given up any pretence of asserting themselves any more, and are simply going through the motions while they wait for retirement, and their pensions, to kick in.

'You want to know what real stress is?' Gordon said to me once when I came home and started to tell him about my problems at ForGiving. 'Working with those kids day after day, not knowing what's going to happen next! Going to work with that morale-sapping feeling of dread in the pit of your stomach - fully aware that as you drive away at the end of yet another disastrous day, you must face them all again the following morning. Wondering if they are going to steal from you, spit on you or knife you!'

Those things - and more - have happened to him during his teaching career. I must accept that this is the way he now thinks. They have finally defeated him. His retirement is stress related; he is a shadow of the man he used to be - there's no fight left in him now - and he's so low that I never even think of mentioning my 'little local difficulties' to him - because there's just no point.

We haven't shared the same bedroom for some time, as Gordon does like to stay up late at night nursing a whisky - or two or three! Over the years, we have settled into a routine where we seem to trouble each other as little as possible.

In the early years of our marriage, Gordon and I used to play a lot of sport together. We played tennis and badminton for a club. He also played squash well, but I could never get the hang of it. Sport was a way of de-stressing, and it worked.

Gordon was always very competitive, and playing sport, not only with me, but with others too, seemed to offer all sorts of benefits, therapeutic and otherwise.

He played rugby to a high standard when he was a young man, and the county caps he was awarded played a part in landing him his first teaching jobs.

Because we all were so bound up in a sporty life, many years ago we turned the basement of our house into a small gym. There he could lift his weights, ride his exercise bike and later we installed the rowing machine. We felt that we had created something that we could all enjoy. I don't use the weights, but I do like to use the exercise bike, and after a few false starts, I began to like the rowing machine too and I use it frequently.

We still enjoy working out in our little gym, I am happy to say. Gordon often pops down there for a few minutes and so do I. It's a shared interest, one of the few that we still have. We don't often use it together, but occasionally I 'buddy' Gordon as he bench-presses his weights. When he sets himself a difficult challenge, I assist him with the 'on and off', helping him to take the strain as the weights are lifted from the stand and on to his chest. And when he has finished, the reverse process happens, as the weights are safely placed back on their stand.

The regular exercise does keep him looking good, and on those occasions recently when he has come home obviously under stress, he has enjoyed power lifting and bench-pressing his way into a more relaxed frame of mind. If I am buddying him, I also like to use the exercise bike while reading a book, leaving him in peace to do his reps, and helping him to replace the weights safely when he has finished.

I have always enjoyed a good workout too, and as I get older, I think that I am beginning to feel the benefit of having looked after my body all these years. Many of the people at ForGiving look old and strained, some well beyond their years. I feel fine, I am delighted to say.

I took up running almost a year ago now, and I am comfortable jogging around the area where we live, and then spending fifteen or twenty-minutes downstairs on the equipment.

Our kids also used to use our gym, but they are now grown up and they flew the nest some time ago. Matthew and Alice have their own lives now, but I feel that the main reason that they have stopped coming home to see us quite so often is because Gordon has become so difficult to be with - even if you love him.

He is so miserable - and angry - all the time, and I am sure it is that which keeps them away from us. I would love to see more of the kids, and of course, I would love to be a grandma, but that hasn't happened - yet.

Alice is twenty-three and now lives near Birmingham with her boyfriend, David. He does something in computers and Alice is a nurse. They say that they have no plans to start a family.

Matthew is twenty-five and lives in the Northern Quarter in Manchester. He left school at sixteen telling us that no, he didn't want to stay on in the sixth form. We were disappointed, of course, but he was adamant, and rather than create a huge amount of resentment, we acquiesced - hoping that at some point he would see sense and get himself an education.

He has had a few different jobs and is now working in the students' union bar at the university. Matthew is gay, and happy being gay, he tells me! I think that I am happy for him too, but I haven't discussed this with Gordon, as I am not at all sure how he would respond. In fact, although he may suspect, I am sure that he does not know - or want to know: his mind is closed to some subjects.

I would love to be able to get some comfort from the children at this time, but I fear that is not going to happen.

And there doesn't seem much room in Gordon's life for other people's problems; his own seem so overwhelming.

I keep my fingers crossed that, come the end of the summer term, Gordon will start to relax a little, and see the exciting possibilities that retiring at fifty-five might offer.

I am hopeful - he was such a lovely man when we first married, and it has been tragic to see him lose so much motivation over the years.

He used to love his work so much! Dealing with difficult children is more of a calling than simply a profession. And until quite recently, Gordon had that calling.

There has been a build-up of incidents over the last year or so which seems to have brought matters to a head, and now I know that part of him can't wait to be free of the school, the kids and the whole education system itself. However, I suspect that a larger part of him resents his being asked to take early retirement.

When he does finish, I want us to celebrate his retirement by buying a motor home or a caravan so that we can get away more often. I hope to explore more of Europe eventually, but my ambition is a little more constrained now. I simply want to see Gordon sitting behind the wheel of our brand-new motor home and smiling. That would be enough to begin with. I've never asked much of life, but now I need to ask a little more of it than I would normally do. I want Gordon back - my Gordon back. And when he does retire, I expect to be saying goodbye to my work at ForGiving at the same time.

***

The police officers left ten minutes ago. A man and a woman; they have been in our sitting room for nearly two hours, talking to Gordon. I have gone into the room to find out what has been going on, and Gordon is sitting there, crying. I have never seen him cry before.

'Gordon, dear. What's happened? What did they want to speak to you about?'

Gordon doesn't even register my presence. He is still crying, but not loud sobs, nothing dramatic. He is quite still, and the tears are the only sign that he is deeply unhappy.

'Is there anything I can ...?'

He turns to me. 'What did you have in mind? What have you ever had in mind?'

'That's not called for, Gordon! Something has happened, and I want to know what it is so that I can help you. Why did those police officers come to our house?'

He takes a paper napkin from the coffee table, then another and then he looks at me.

'Someone has made an accusation.'

'Someone? Who? What kind of accusation?'

'One of the boys has accused me of assault.'

'Who is it, Gordon?'

'I don't know. They wouldn't say. It's not one of the kids at school now. It's from years ago.'

'How long ago?'

'They wouldn't tell me that either. They are not from round here, they're part of a team looking into historical cases of abuse.'

'What do you mean?'

'You know damn well what I mean! Jimmy Savile - remember him? He started it.'

'You didn't know Jimmy Savile - did you?'

'For Christ's sake, woman! Of course, I didn't know him! But he started all this.'

'You've lost me.'

Gordon can be quite unpleasant when he is angry. He's not violent, not like that - no, he becomes sarcastic, even to me. I don't approve of that kind of behaviour from anyone, especially him, so I am choosing not to provoke him too far.

'If you want to tell me, tell me,' I say. 'If you don't, that's all right by me too. I am here to help if I can. That's all.'

There is a silence, longer than most of our silences - which can be quite long - and then Gordon says, 'This Jimmy Savile thing opened the floodgates, it seems. All kinds of nonsense is being dredged up from the past because some of our former pupils - or the ambulance chasers who are representing them - see money signs, compensation.

'Some boy has alleged that I assaulted him, another boy says that I dislocated his finger.'

'And did you?'

'Probably did. If the kid was big and angry and had gone ape-shit on me, if I needed to stop something violent from happening, I would always go for the little finger. That helped me get control.'

He continues, 'It's not assault, though! It's regaining control - only that. If some kid has become dangerous, you can't 'talk them down'. They're a danger - not only to you - but to themselves.'

'And you did this?'

'Probably. I say probably, because I can't remember an incident when I hurt anyone, but I doubt if that matters. Anybody, any former pupil can say anything they want - and they will be believed because of all these old rockers, the DJs and the rest - and what they did to kids who came near them.'

'But you are a teacher, Gordon, not a DJ.'

'I know that - I suspect the police know that too, but the officer said that they were 'duty-bound to follow up on any allegations, no matter how tenuous they may be.''

'Tenuous! They're not tenuous at all. It might not have been you who was involved, but you've often come home and told me of some of the things that have gone on.

'You've had to sack people before - remember that man who punched one of the kids who spat on him?'

'The policewoman told me that their team is interviewing several people from the school, past and present members of staff - teachers and care workers.'

'So, it's not just you?'

'Not 'just' me? It's not 'even' me. I'm not involved.   That's what I told them. I said that on the rare occasions when I came upon any 'troubling' activity, I acted. And since I became headmaster, that's what I have done.'

'So, you've nothing to worry about, have you? It's routine. They had to ask you some questions, but that's probably that.'

Gordon seems calmer now. He has stopped crying - maybe a good sign - and possibly he sees the sense in what I have said to him.

'Would you like a cup of tea - or something stronger?' Gordon knows that I don't often suggest 'something stronger', and he smiles. 'Something stronger would be perfect, thank you. I'll go and clean myself up first.' And he does. I pour him a glass of whisky, add a touch of water as he likes it like that, and I wait for him to come back downstairs.

Do you know what I am thinking now? I should be ashamed of myself, I know, but what I find myself thinking is what would those people who work at ForGiving make of all this, if it got out?

***

When I do come in to ForGiving on the Monday morning, the gossip is of a different kind. It was all over the news apparently, but we missed it what with Gordon and his problems, and his whisky - and the fact that he finished off the bottle and became quite offensive towards me, so he had to take me up to Silloth for the day on Sunday and be very, very kind to me all day - the gossip is not about us.

Joyce Todd, one of the volunteers - she works on a Friday, so I don't see her, but we have met to say hello once or twice - Christmas lunch and so on. Anyway, she has been murdered! On Friday - that's why she didn't come in, and what's even more surprising is that the police have arrested Mickey Hembrow. Apparently, he worked her shift on Friday morning because he happened to be in Ambleton. He is the shy, strange looking man who comes in once or twice a week - lives in Winstermere. He's nice, not exactly my sort, but always polite, and he seems quite gentle. To be frank, he looks a bit uncared for. I have always thought that he is the exact kind of person who would benefit from a makeover on one of those TV programmes, but I would never suggest such a thing.

That's why Desmond said Mickey won't be coming in! And, of course, neither will Joyce - obviously. I can't believe that Mickey is a killer, though - it must be a mistake.

I am listening to and looking at three ladies who work with us and have come in for a chat and to recount their understanding of the situation.

Apparently, Joyce was attacked and suffocated with a Co-op bag! And Mickey's fingerprints were on the bag that had been used to suffocate Joyce. All that was on the television news, but Gordon and I missed that too.

Although I am listening carefully to what these ladies are saying, my radar is also trying to pick up other signals, signals that are now more important to me than whether Mickey did or did not commit a murder. Yes, I know that's an important thing to consider - and no, I've never had anything to do with a murder before, and I realise how shocking the event is, but today I am primarily concerned to know whether news of Gordon and his meeting with the police has filtered down to the ladies of ForGiving.

I am relieved that through their eye contact and gestures, the three of them involve me quite naturally into their conversation, and the signals that I am looking for simply don't appear. There is nothing in their demeanour that suggests anything about Gordon and me, about the police speaking to him, or anything that might suggest suspicion or embarrassment.

I am also delighted that I am not the centre of this gossip; a little concerned for Mickey, of course, not that I like him - but he is so ineffectual, despite the way he looks, that I would bet my house that he is not the person who committed this awful crime.

Next week's rota is going to be a bit of a challenge too! Apparently, Monica won't be coming in either. She hopes to be appointed new manager to replace Desmond and Donna, and she must attend a selection course for a couple of days.   To my mind, that's simply an expensive interview, but what do I know?

I think that Monica will be an excellent manager, but I also remember saying that about Desmond, until I realised the truth.

A lot of changes are going to happen here.

***

Our lives have been ripped apart - completely shredded! Gordon has been charged with seven counts of assault against three boys and has been suspended from the school with immediate effect! The alleged offences occurred over ten years ago, it would seem. He is to appear in the magistrates' court next week, and his solicitor says that he is likely to be remanded on bail until he appears at the Crown Court at some future date - but there is also a chance that he could be remanded in custody.

Five former and current members of staff, all people that Gordon has worked with, are also being prosecuted.   Gordon told me this last night, and he said that it would be all over the TV and newspapers from today.

And it is! A reporter from ITV Border came to our house this morning asking for an interview. The telephone has been ringing all morning too - all newspapers and TV people, I think, although there were a couple of silent calls too.

Gordon is not at home. He went out for a long walk early this morning and hasn't returned yet. I was quite unprepared to speak to anyone, and slightly annoyed that Gordon had left me on my own. I was sensible enough (I think) not to open the door, and they did go away when it became obvious that I was not willing to speak to them. I dread watching the local news this evening.

And the very thing I dreaded most has happened! The six o'clock local news had the school as its first item. They named Gordon as the head teacher and then they listed all the other five men who were charged. Three teachers, two care assistants and my Gordon all have been charged with a total of twenty-five offences!

Gordon and I watched the news together. When he came back to the house, it was late afternoon, and to tell you the truth, I was beginning to be concerned for him. However, he did return - bringing all the newspapers with him - he had been to the village. He also smelled quite strongly of alcohol, so I could easily deduce where he had spent most of the afternoon!

And there is no getting away from it! Gordon's school has also been mentioned in all the major newspapers. Our local paper, the Westmorland Gazette, doesn't come out until Friday, but I can imagine that this story will be on the front page.

None of the newspapers gave out our full addresses, but they all mentioned the towns or villages where we I live.

It's out there now, and there is nothing I can do to mitigate things. Gordon seems devastated - the funny thing is that on this occasion, I would have preferred him to be angry. But he's still and silent. He watched everything on all the TV news channels. Channel Four news made no mention, but ITV Border and BBC North West both went to town - reporters outside the school, the full names of all the accused, and a special potted biography of Gordon himself - something which we could well have done without.

It has all become so - so brittle! I am finding it difficult to describe how I feel, what I want to happen now, and how I should behave, both to Gordon and to the outside world.

We have been married for a long time, and at this moment I have no idea what I should say to Gordon. My mind is totally blank.

I ought to say something to the children, let them know - then again, should I? What will I say? How will I say it? I will have to be careful not to pre-judge anything, although I suspect that our children might do exactly that.

Something that truly eats away at me while I am thinking about how to approach this issue with Matthew and Alice is that I simply don't know how they might respond. I ought to know; after all, they are our children and I thought that I was close to them, but over the last few years a gap has opened; there's no denying it.

With Matthew particularly, I fear that he will find it difficult to support his dad. I don't even think that he will want to - sad, I know. He knows that Gordon feels ambivalent towards him. As a result, whenever we do see Matthew, he is always so defensive, and it seems that he can't wait to get away from us.

For a long time, I had meant to sit down with Gordon and sort things out. Matthew being gay is something that we should have learned to accept. All I have ever wanted is a happy son, but Gordon has never wanted to know. Put simply, put like that, you can see my problem. If Gordon doesn't want to know, if, like a normal kind of dad, he had found it difficult to cope with a gay son, I might well have been able to understand. So, I suspect that he simply pretends that everything is normal, and if nothing is mentioned, there is nothing to worry about.

I should have done something about this a long time ago, but this is certainly not the time to open yet another can of worms.

And even with Alice, I have sensed that she doesn't find being with us a warm - or loving - experience. Maybe it is me, and I am over-dramatising things, but she was such a happy kid, always laughing. I rarely see her laughing now. In fact, I rarely see her, full stop.

I'll wait to hear from them - they are bound to see something on the TV - the amount of coverage there has been. If, after a few days, I've not heard anything, I'll reassess.

However, one thing I am sure of is this: the news is out there now, all of it. Well, not exactly all of it. When the trial comes along, there will be a lot of detail, and a lot of embarrassment for everyone. And what if Gordon has done these things? What will happen if he is found guilty?

For example, if the charges related to physical assault, or if they were about sexual assault – would you react differently? I think that I would. 'Seven counts of assault', that's what Gordon has been charged with. I have tried asking him to give me some more information - some insight into what he has been charged with. But he always seems to swat me away.   His excuse, because that is what I think it is - his excuse is that he can't remember the incidents mentioned in the charges.

I could almost accept that he might have lashed out in anger at some time or other. There is no doubt that all the staff at the school are frequently provoked, and the possibility of a violent reaction is always there.

Sometimes children must be restrained, and restraint can be thought of as a form of assault: a young man might resent being held down by force, and later in life, he might seek to get some form of revenge on the person who restrained him.

But if these are sexual offences? If Gordon has been charged with sexual offences against these children, how should I respond? This whole thing is so far beyond my sense of understanding, so beyond the questions I thought that my life would ask of me. There's no logical conclusion I can think of, and that's my dilemma.

Apart from one thing! I know how I will respond if it were to turn out that Gordon has been abusing children in a sexual way. If that is the case, there will be no more Gordon in my life. And part of me is beginning to believe that he knows that.

***

The Mickey and Joyce murder thing has been a godsend! I mean no disrespect, but all the goings on in that story have been the main topic of conversation everywhere, and my little local difficulties have not been high on anyone's agenda.   And for that, I am most grateful.

Mickey was released from custody. He wasn't the person who murdered Joyce. We all expect that he will be coming back to work in ForGiving. We are all walking rather stiff-legged around that idea of course, but we also seem to be avoiding any kind of discussion about who did kill her.

What this does mean is that there is somebody - a murderer - who is still out there. If this person has an agenda, he might still be tempted to carry it out.

And why would anyone want to kill Joyce? She was lovely! She was always smiling, always wanting the best for ForGiving and for the volunteers. If anyone knew that they couldn't make it for their shift for whatever reason, Joyce was the first person that they would contact. Nobody took advantage of her; she was simply always willing to help.

Of course, that is looking at her from a ForGiving perspective. What if Joyce had a 'back story'? Did she have a secret existence in a previous life that brought about her violent death in such a terrifying way? There has been a lot of speculation, and I am as guilty as anyone; we all love juicy gossip, and nothing is juicier than something like this.

I think that we, Gordon, Matthew Alice and me, are exceptional as a family in that we have lived in the area for many years. Most of my ForGiving colleagues, however, will have left something behind - they have chosen to remove themselves from where they have lived, often for decades, so that they can retire up here. I know that is a broad generalisation, but so many people whom I know and relate to - have done just that, and who's to say that Joyce didn't leave something unsavoury behind? She was a very reserved person and gave no clues. As far as I can tell, none of us knew much about her and what brought her to the Lakes.

As I am finding out to my cost, many ordinary relationships seem to be built on truly flimsy foundations, and what I always thought of as my strong and stable family is as unstable and liable to crash to earth as that of anybody else.

Small consolation: we live near Sizergh, a little outside of Kendal. It's far enough from Ambleton for me not to be involved in too much gossip, and far enough from Churchfield, where Gordon's school is, for us to keep under the radar - I hope! We do have a few neighbours, but we don't have much to do with them. They are all quite elderly: in these circumstances, that might turn out to be a blessing!

***

Matthew came up to see me yesterday - he knew that Gordon was not in the house, because he phoned me to check. Gordon is rarely in the house these days, but on this occasion, I knew exactly where he was. He and his fellow defendants had all been asked to meet the solicitors who were going to represent them at the trial.

I hadn't seen Matthew for about six months, since late December, when I went to see him in Manchester. That was the third time that he hadn't turned up for Christmas, and it was no longer a surprise - it has become a new, if slightly unwelcome, tradition.

'You've lost a lot of weight, Matt.' My first words were stating the obvious as he is stick thin.

'Exercise - and I've gone veggie. James is veggie, and it's much easier.' I know of James, James is the man he lives with. James is his partner. I didn't pursue the topic as there is no need. Matthew and I have been through all that.

'We don't see much of you now, dear. Are you busy all the time?'

'It's all a bit embarrassing, Mum - the James thing, and so on. I know my dad doesn't want to discuss anything like that, so if I do speak to him, it's like a huge part of my life has to be blocked out of any conversation.'

'He'll come around, I'm sure.'

Matthew frowns. 'He won't. He's a position to defend, especially now.'

'What do you mean?'

'You've no idea, have you?'

My body temperature seems to plummet - I am freezing cold, and I don't know why.

'Alice won't come back home either.'

'Alice?' It's true. Alice is quite chatty when I talk to her on the phone, but she always seems to avoid coming up here. Not even at Christmas.

'There is a reason,' Matthew continues, 'And that's why I am here. With all of this going on - Dad and the school - I've decided that this is the time. I've talked to Alice; she's not happy, but I said I'd do it anyway.'

'Do what anyway? What do you mean you have talked to Alice? About what?'

Matthew does that thing of playing with his hair - he is a ten-year-old again - except that he is no longer a child. He will soon be twenty - six and he lives with his gay partner James in a flat in Manchester. He is nervous, and raises his head to look at me - to catch my eye deliberately.

'Dad used to come into our rooms late at night.'

***

I have lived a tranquil life. I am not an emotional person and I have tried to be a good wife as well as a good mother. I have failed on both counts: that explosion in my brain is the proof. I have failed to protect my children.

For years, I worked hard at our marriage, despite the obvious way in which it was sliding downhill. Gordon's dismissive approach to anything I do or say should have prompted me to rethink things. I saw it differently: I saw it as a challenge to get things back to where I thought they were - once.

I have always been able to accept, even excuse - forgive me for saying that - his way of talking down to me, his increasingly short tempers - and those long, brooding silences. I was prepared to excuse them because I saw myself, and my failings as his wife, as the reason for Gordon's seeming dissatisfaction with me.

It was motivation - motivation for me to do better, motivation to find a new combination, a new and better way of relating to him.

I was even stupid enough to believe that buying a camper van when Gordon retired would be a way of fixing things between us. God, was I deluded! The only reason I would think of getting a camper van now would be so that I could run the bastard down with it!

***

Matthew has gone back to Manchester - to his home: he left as soon as he could. He had prepared a speech, and he had plucked up enough courage to come up to see me and deliver it. But not enough courage to allow me to question him during it. He wanted to get it out first - and then, he said, he would see if he could discuss anything.

It wasn't a conversation, so what he did say was as if a huge lorry had pulled up and tipped its contents on to our drive. Matthew didn't want to spend a moment longer in the house than he had to - too many memories - his words!

He's left me sitting here, alone and completely bereft; everything unravelled. Yes, I should have known, yes, I should have been able to protect them. Yes, it explains why both he and Alice stopped coming to see us.

But it does not explain why I did not know. As he was getting up to go, I asked Matthew why he never once said anything. And Alice! Little Alice who has now become such a stranger to me. Why did she not say anything?

'You should have known, Mum.'

'How?'

'You are our mum! The signals were all there. And you didn't pick up on them. I didn't know what to say - or how to say it. He's my dad. He said that he loved me. You must have seen it in Alice too - her weird eating habits, and then she was cutting herself, running away. It was all there for you to see.'

'I thought that it was typical teenage behaviour! Dad said he came across it all the time at school. I never thought. Why didn't you say? Why didn't you tell me?'

'What would you have done? What could you have done? I knew - I'm not speaking for Alice here - I don't know why she never said anything, but I knew that if I did, the family would break up - disintegrate. I suppose I thought that it was better keeping quiet. At least we remained living as a family.

'And I was frightened! I was frightened of what Dad would do to us if you found out. He kept on making me promise, promise that I wouldn't tell. He always would say that if I did tell anyone, I would end up going to a school like his! I knew enough about that school to know what he meant.'

'How long did this go on?' I'm asking this question almost in the same way as I would ask someone about the weather. I'm filling a space in my mind, that's all. I have no idea what to say, or how to progress this conversation in any way that won't bring more disaster into my home, into my world. Then he answers, and the next bomb explodes, and this time it is nuclear.

'It started when I was five or six.'

'What? Jesus! Matthew, Matthew!' I want to die. A combination of feelings that I can't define, but all of which are mixing together - a malign, amorphous cloud enveloping me - fear, revulsion, a striking awareness of my own culpability in all this - 'I have no idea what to say to you, my darling,' is the best I can come out with. A bland statement of the bleeding obvious. At this, the most dramatic moment in my life, the exact moment - where I am weighing my contribution to this family - and finding it entirely wanting, I resort to clichés and the tacit admission that I too, would also have been helpless.

Matthew is standing at the doorway, itching to get away, but he compounds things by completing the equation for me.

'And you wouldn't have been able to do anything either. You have always been a loving mum, but in our family, that wasn't enough. It should have been, but it wasn't. I don't think that I understood what was happening - and I had no idea how to explain it to myself. Then he started on Alice - and I knew how wrong it was.

'I was about ten or eleven when he stopped using me, but Alice never said anything - I assumed. He wasn't interested in me anymore, and as Alice's behaviour became more and more erratic, I started to understand.'

Again, I try - I have been so out of it - redundant, both in this conversation, and in all that has gone on in my house - under my eyes! I am trying to get some sense of it, some slight understanding, any foothold to help me say something worthwhile.

And then I say the stupidest thing I have ever said in my life. It just comes out, 'And is that why you became gay, darling?'

Matthew doesn't answer me directly, but his eyes tell me that I have confirmed it: his perception of me is spot-on.

After a moment or two, he looks at me and says, 'It doesn't work like that, Mum. I thought you'd know. I'd better go now. James and I are going to a concert tonight at the Bridgewater Hall.'

'What do you want me to do, Matthew?'

'No idea. What's there to do? It will all come out. There is a pattern here, what with what's been going on at the school.'

'You don't think your dad has been ...?'

Matthew gives me another of those long, sad looks, his lovely, loving eyes looking at me in the way I remember he did as a little boy.

'Mum, I know what he did to me - and Alice.' That look again, and then he goes. He gives me a kiss, and he puts his arms around me, but not with any warmth - or any love. It's a formality, nothing more. Then he leaves. His car is outside, he gets into it and starts the engine. He doesn't look at me or at the house. I think that I can see tears on his face, or at least, he wipes something away, but that is all. He drives off - mirror, signal, manoeuvre, exactly as I taught him - and he doesn't look back.

**

During the last awful week or so, I have immersed myself in my work at ForGiving. I have taken on two extra days and filled in for anyone who was unable to do their shift, morning or afternoon. I even suggested to Monica that when she takes over, we open on Sundays - and that I was happy to run the shop if she felt that it was a good idea.

I have been out running, or at least my version of running - shuffling is probably a more accurate word - every morning and most evenings. I also spend longer out at the shops than I have ever done before, and I walk wherever I can, rather than take my car.

Several people have congratulated me on what they see as my new lifestyle. But of course, it is nothing of the sort. These are simply displacement activities, and they have become so vital to me to help preserve my sanity. These activities, and many more, deflect me from the searing images that plague me whenever my mind has a moment spare.

At ForGiving, they all know what's happened at Gordon's school - probably more than I do! There was quite a lot of guarded whispering to begin with, but quite suddenly, the atmosphere changed.

I think they now see that I am a victim too! Most of the ladies have been solicitous - part of me suspects that they might be trying to glean additional insights from me via this approach - but their kindness, for the most part, is real and sincere. I have been able to take a lot of comfort from that.

Desmond, the manager at ForGiving, and Donna his little bossy wife, are leaving soon; 'moving on' is the term that Desmond uses. Curiously, they are the only people who have been unpleasant to me. They have cut me dead! This is difficult to do in a small shop, but they manage it perfectly. I now receive messages and communications via a third party, usually one of the ladies - all of whom realise how ridiculously D&D are behaving. So, it's quite amusing, in its own way. It could be wounding, but because none of us takes their opinions seriously anymore, it doesn't seem to matter what they think - or say - in that snide way of theirs.

A small example: The daybook is where we write notes to each other, so that the next shift can see what is happening and what needs to be done. We all use first names, and always have done. D&D have written three notes to me, and they have used my first name - Julia - and my surname! That little touch of passive-aggression did not go unnoticed. The next day someone had put a smiley face next to the notes, and later someone wrote 'Someone has been VERY naughty' next to one of them.

I feel so much better - the ladies are on my side, and that matters more than I could possibly have thought it would.

Meanwhile Gordon goes about his days in a constant blur. He spends a lot of time out 'walking' - I think that means the pub, and I know he often takes a flask of whisky in his pocket too!

When at home, he is spending much more time downstairs in the gym. I suppose he's trying to see if the 'healthy body, healthy mind' thing is going to work.   Personally, I doubt it will.

He continues his exercise routines, but no longer seems to require my 'buddy' services - not that he would get them if he asked!

I have to keep as far away from him as I possibly can, and he has settled in to this new mode of our relationship without even noticing the change. He must know, mustn't he? He must know how much I loathe him now.

From whenever I wake up - never mind the cold sweat wakings-up that occur most nights - but in the morning, from my first conscious moment, I am thinking about Gordon with Matthew, Gordon with Alice, for God's sake, and now Gordon with anonymous children from his school.

And even though those images of Gordon with children from the school are anonymous, they are as unsettling as the pictures I conjure up of my own children being abused by their father.

My most frequent dream concerns my kids, when they were kids, and I am in a room watching them. Gordon is with them. There is a glass screen - like you see on those TV detective programmes where they interview the witnesses. But I can't communicate - I am hammering on the screen and screaming at them, but I can't help them, I can't be their mum - I can only watch!

A few years ago, I was listening to a radio phone-in when a woman came on. She said that at that moment, her husband was taking a bath with his twelve-year-old daughter. She asked the radio presenter if that was normal behaviour.

I, and I imagine thousands of other people, screamed 'No! No! No! The man's a pervert! Call the police!' I knew it was wrong, I knew it was abusive, and yet I have been oblivious to similar things that were going on in my family for years.

I should go to the police, no messing, and no more procrastination. But should I ask my children first? Would Matthew and Alice be prepared to testify? They've kept it all so quiet for so long that I am not sure that they would.

In the meantime, I continue to distance myself from Gordon. That's not too difficult, as he is obviously preoccupied with the trial, and with being noticed or pointed at almost whenever he goes out. At least, that's what he told me during one of our increasingly rare conversations. He's probably overstating things, a touch of paranoia. I doubt whether many people know him by sight, and those around us already know about the court case.

It is true that many of our friends and acquaintances seem to have slipped overboard and away, but frankly, I don't miss them at all. The ladies at ForGiving have helped me through this more than some people whom we have known for over twenty years.

***

I spoke to Alice on the phone a couple of days ago. After our usual polite, dancing around; the sanitised chat about our curiously ideal circumstances (everything is always absolutely fine here, and ditto with Alice), I asked her if she had seen anything about her dad's school in the newspaper.

'Of course, I have.'

'Do you want to talk about it, darling?' I hoped that I was being genuinely helpful.

'Talk about what?'

'You know - about you, and the things Dad did to you.'

'What?'

'Matthew told me.'

'Matthew should have kept his bloody mouth shut!' Alice's retort surprises me, but I try again.

'I know it's difficult, darling. Shall I come down to Birmingham? We could have a coffee together, and maybe talk some things through.'

'Talk some things through? You're a counsellor now, are you? A bit late for that, don't you think?'

'Alice, I knew nothing about it. I had no idea.'

'You should have known! You watched me - you watched me fall apart! I've still got scars all down my arms, Mum!'

'I was naïve and stupid, Alice. I tried to explain this to Matthew. I wanted to do something, but your dad kept telling me that it would pass. Lots of children go through phases.   He said that if I confronted you, it could make things worse, and I believed him.'

'Ha!'

'I want to make it right now, Alice, if I can. I love you so much - and I know it's late, and I also know you are trying to make sense of things - but I want to help you. I need to make sense of things too!'

'It's too late! You can't do anything now. I know it wasn't your fault, but I also know that there is more that you should have done. Now I can cope - I am in control and I'm happier now than I have ever been. I want to keep it that way. I enjoy the work that I am doing, and David is a good man - I love being with him.

'I can't tell him all that happened, not yet. But I will - one day. He knows that there is something wrong with me; I'm slowly getting closer to him, and he realises that I have issues that I must work through. He says that he is prepared to wait.   I hope that's true - I believe it, and I feel safe with him.'

'I am so pleased to hear that,' I reply. 'That's all I ever wanted - for you to be happy.'

'So, stay away, Mum. I don't want you to come to Birmingham, ok? I mean it!'

'But Alice, I want to try to make it up to you - I know I've failed you, and I can't leave it at that.'

'If you come to Birmingham, I won't meet you and I will never speak to you again - do you hear me? Is that clear?'

I do hear her, and it is clear, but I have nothing to say by way of an answer. There is no point anyway, because Alice has put the phone down, and I dare not call her back.

**

I have been out for a run - my third today! Living near Sizergh is perfect for me as a jogger. I can run for miles without seeing anyone. I hate it if I see someone coming towards me because I have to keep on running, pretending that I am not breathing too heavily - until I pass them by or the car goes around a bend or a corner.

I am aware that there is something faintly ludicrous about all of this. The unflattering Lycra, the headband, the water bottle with the isotonics - all the things that made me smile when I used to be a bystander, and I watched the anorexic obsessives pounding out the miles. Now I am one of them. I run between four and six miles, sometimes three times a day.

I feel like the character whose name we used for our own daughter, Alice.
'–so long as I get SOMEWHERE,' Alice added as an explanation.
'Oh, you're sure to do that,' said the Cat, 'if you only walk long enough.'

Well, I have walked long enough - I have mostly run - and then I have repeated the process time and time again, but there is still no destination in sight.

Nothing from either Matthew or our Alice since our last embarrassing conversations. Because of what Alice said, I have not dared to call her. I had rather hoped that Matthew would get back to me - we do still have a bond, I am sure of that, and I am clinging on to that hope. That's me in desperation - although the 'Mrs Sensible' in me has admitted that it might be receding.

I have lost my children - the two people in my life who truly matter to me, and I don't have the skills, I don't have the intelligence, and I don't think that I have the nerve to do anything about it.

I go into the kitchen for a drink - taking on board some fluid - as I would say in my own tiny jogger's world, a world which now revolves around distances run, brands of trainers worn, support bandages, sports watches: T S Eliot had Prufrock measuring out his life with coffee spoons. My life is now measured by Fitbit readings! Then the even more ridiculous stuff: 'sports drinks' - yes, I have found myself exploring the full range of options from *Lucozade* – crazy! And we mustn't forget 'jogger's nipple', something I always thought was an urban myth until I experienced it! It's real, and so are the special creams and devices you can get to ward it off. It is a different world, I tell you!

Because of this lifestyle change, I have lost about five kilos, so I feel pretty smug. This evening, my Fitbit tells me that tonight I have burned off two hundred and thirty-seven calories! I am proud to be the parody that I have become - this is the new me!

Gordon is downstairs in the gym. The whooshing sound of his new rowing machine, the 'Concept 2' - I like using that machine too - has just been replaced by the more solid metallic clunks of his weights. He is loading up the bar bell for his bench-pressing: that has always been his favourite exercise.

I am slightly miffed now, as I had thought that I might do thirty minutes or so on the machines. I decide to put it off until he has finished, and I lie down on the floor and begin to do some stretching exercises; some of the moves I have learned in Pilates.

A few minutes later I hear Gordon's voice, 'Are you there, Julia?'

'What is it? What do you want?' I reply.

'Would you mind helping me? I thought I'd try for 130.   I've been working up to it. Could you buddy me this once?'

Buddying Gordon is the last thing I want to do, but I rationalise my response by saying to myself that the sooner he has finished his reps, the sooner he will go, and I can get on with my own thirty minutes down there.

'OK,' I say. 'Give me a minute or two.' There is no reason why I should not go down there immediately, other than my reluctance to jump to attention when he calls me.

After much more than a minute or two, and my stretching exercises over, I get up from the floor and make my way downstairs.

'What do you want me to do?'

'Just 'off' me, please. It's a bit heavy to risk it.'

Gordon is lying on his back, on the bench. I must say that he looks pretty good there. His arms and pecs are well developed, his hands are grasping the barbell, waiting for me to help him 'off' it from its stand so he can thrust it upwards.

I stand in my normal position, at his head and facing him. Together we lift the barbell, and as Gordon begins his reps, I gradually release the weights from my grip.

He is now bench-pressing one hundred and thirty kilos - thirty kilos above his body weight, and very impressive for a fifty-odd year old headteacher about to take early retirement.

He does five or six reps and then he slows down as it becomes more difficult.

'Right love, that's me. Can you help me 'on' them now?'

I reach down to take hold of the weights in the same way as I normally do. This time I don't help him lift. I push down. Gordon is caught by surprise, and the bar, with its weights attached at either end, drops across his throat.

Because of the way he is lying, he can't move the barbell from his throat. He bends and twists his body, his legs and hips bucking, his arms flailing, but the combined weight of the barbells and of me is simply too much for him to overcome.

After what, for me, is a frighteningly long time, his flailing weakens, and then I see the sign. His eyes cloud over, and I know that he is dying.

When I was a child on the farm, one way I was taught to kill chickens was to catch one by putting a laundry basket over it. Then, by lifting the basket a little, the chicken would try to escape. Forcing the edge of the laundry basket over its neck, and applying pressure to it, would see the chicken die quite quickly. The sign of success was the whiteness in the eyes.

Gordon is now looking straight at me through white eyes.

I am not gloating; in fact, I am surprised at how calm and unmoved I feel. I have righted a wrong. I leave Gordon as he is, and I go back upstairs.

Before I do anything else, I reset my Fitbit watch to the correct time. It has been set one hour ahead since I bought it, and I have been meaning to correct it for ages.

Now that I have done that, and if anybody asks, it would appear that I was out running while Gordon had such an unfortunate accident.

He should have waited for his buddy!

Desmond and Donna

It's about a quarter to seven on a Saturday night at ForGiving, the Lake District charity shop, when Desmond suddenly turns to his wife who is sitting next to him as they both try to reconcile the shop's till - yet again.

'You know, I've had enough of this. It's a simple till; you should get it right every time. There's only been two of us on it. What's happening? Can you think of any mistake you made?'

'Me?' Donna seems as frustrated by this as Desmond. 'Why would it be me? You've used it as often as I have - and it was you who messed it up last time.'

'Twenty-six pounds and thirty pence up. Bollocks! I'll leave it until Monday. We've been here long enough. This is eating into our weekend.'

It has been a frustrating day for Desmond and for Donna. They both came in to work this morning a few minutes after nine o'clock, ready to open the shop at ten. They have been the only people working all day, so that meant no lunch break.

Desmond has been the manager at ForGiving for almost three years, and Donna comes in with him almost every time he is on duty. She doesn't enjoy working in the shop but wants to keep an eye on him - just in case. She probably doesn't have an answer to the question, 'Just in case - what?', but something at the back of her mind convinces her that it is better to be safe than sorry.

And now she is needed. Over the last few months, the number of volunteers they can depend upon has reduced. This is the reason they are here now, the shop manager and his wife, poring over the till roll, trying to see where the error occurred. They can't get anyone to work on a Saturday, and to cap it all, Patsy, the regional manager, has sent an email asking Desmond to make sure that he can staff the shop to open on Sundays from the beginning of next month.

'Look at this! Sunday opening! Who the hell does she expect to work on a Sunday?'

'You - and me, obviously. The volunteers won't work Saturdays; they are hardly going to come on Sundays, are they? Anyway, they'll all be at church.' Donna has put all the cash into the night safe bag, has gathered up her coat, her handbag and one or two items of clothing that she has taken a fancy to. She'll try them on at home and bring them back next week if she doesn't like them.

Desmond's frustration boils over, 'Well, they can spin! You know what? Why don't we pack it all in? There's no money in it; it's supposed to be a part-time job, but I seem to be doing more and more each month. I should never have taken it on. I don't enjoy it, and there are so many more interesting things that we should be doing with our lives. I think that we should up and go - let Monica take over.'

Monica has been angling for the manager's job for some time, and Desmond is aware of this. So is Donna, and she's asking herself if he does resign, what the hell is he going to do?

They check that all the windows are closed, switch off the lights and lock the shop up. The day's takings go into the night safe at the bank around the corner - the last bank remaining in the village. What is going to happen when that branch closes - as it will - is anybody's guess.

Now, Desmond and Donna have finished for this week. They haven't discussed it, but the chances are that each of them knows what they would rather do this evening, and that is nothing more than a stiff gin and tonic and a quiet evening in front of the TV. That's not going to happen, though. They will be out to a dinner party - for which they are already running late - as their busy social calendar is the single most important matter in their lives.

On the short drive to their home on a small estate on the outskirts of Ambleton - they could walk, but never do - Donna is thinking about their last conversation. So, Desmond wants to walk away from yet another job? She knows, as she assumes, does he, that this is something that he simply can't afford to do. Yet Donna knows more than anyone else that her husband is capable of making flaky choices on a regular basis. Their life has been full of them.

The last few years have not been easy. Desmond used to work in a local school, and he took voluntary redundancy from his job as a lab technician about ten years ago. The small lump sum he received is long gone, and his tiny pension is way below what they need to live on.

Donna knows this: she is currently unemployed - apart from her voluntary work at ForGiving. She left her last job 'helping out' in a café because of a disagreement. She has had many jobs during the time that they have lived in the Lakes, but all of them have been of the minimum wage variety, and sadly, because she has no qualifications to speak of apart from a basic hygiene certificate, the chances of her earning enough money to keep the household herself, are minimal - and she has no pension, either!

So, he must keep this job! She can't allow him to throw it away in a fit of pique - like he has done so many times before - because neither of them is young enough to be able to start again.

Desmond is going on seventy for God's sake! He behaves as if he were thirty-five. There are some areas where Donna would prefer him to be thirty-five, but this is not one of them. He took this job, not because it's a choice he has made, 'putting something back'; he's working because he must. The bills, their expensive social life, and their frequent holidays - at least one a month, a few days away when they can 'relax', these are vital elements to the lives they have chosen, and they can't be jettisoned because Desmond is annoyed with something.

She goes for it: 'You can't resign from the job, and you know it. So please, don't do anything stupid.'

There, she's said it, and even after over forty years of marriage, she is not sure of the response she is going to get.

They are turning into their street now, and Desmond has not said a word. He continues to drive - and suddenly the silence is screaming at them.

This is what Donna hates the most, and why she tries to avoid this kind of situation whenever the potential for it flares up. She has never been able to negotiate – to discuss, to insist - on anything. Desmond has always made the decisions - all of them.

They have arrived home. The engine is switched off and Desmond opens his car door and gets out. He moves towards the house assuming that Donna will follow.

She does not. He turns towards her, noticing that she has made no move at all to get out of the car.

'What's the matter with you? Come on. We're out again in thirty minutes. If you want a shower, you'd better get moving.'

Donna makes no reply. She continues to sit in the car, staring ahead of her. Desmond moves to her side of the car and opens the door.

'I said, if you want a shower...'

'I heard you.' No eye contact, barely acknowledging him, but shaking like a leaf. Desmond notices this. He has seen this sign before, many times.

'Come on Dee,' he's using her pet name to chivvy her along a bit, 'We mustn't be late. We're never late when we go out. You know that.'

'You go.' She's still staring ahead, still refusing to look at him, 'I'll stay here. I don't fancy going out anyway.'

'I can't go by myself, Dee. Come on, let's get changed. You'll feel better after a shower.'

'I'm not going anywhere - it's another expensive bottle of wine, another long car journey. Another evening of lies and pretence with people who don't even like us - and we don't like either, and I'm sick of it. I'm sitting here looking at us running out of money - going bust, and then to cap it all, you are about to give up the only job you have.'

'I'll find something else.'

'What, exactly? What will you do? You've got an executive position in your fantasy world, have you? Head-hunters chasing after you, are they? Forget the lies. Be realistic for once!'

'What the hell has got into you? This is not what I expect.   Get out of the car now, please!'

Donna is still shaking, and now there are tears as well.

She looks at him for the first time since they got into the car. This is the man she has lived with for a lifetime. This is the man she hitched her star to at the age of fourteen when she first saw him in the lab at school. It was the white coat that did it, she remembers - and he was so tall! She's never been keen on white since. And it was not a star that she hitched herself to. If anything, it was a plain piece of rock, a sad old meteorite which had burned up in the atmosphere. There is nothing left of it now. Nothing at all. Apart from the gas - obviously. He's at that age.

'Desmond, I'm not going anywhere.'

'Oh yes you are!' Desmond opens the door of the car and tries to pull her out. The seat belt prevents any movement, so he leans in and undoes the belt, exactly as one would do with a child or an elderly relative.

As he does this, Donna bites her husband's ear, causing him to rear backwards, striking the back of his head on the door frame of the car.

'Owww!!! What the hell did you do that for, you stupid bitch!' Desmond stands back from the car and rubs the back of his head. His ear is also bleeding; he now notices blood on his hand, and he can feel it dripping on to his neck. He knows that it will now be staining his shirt.

Donna gets out of the car, 'It's your own fault! You won't listen, will you? You go off into one of your long silences and think that's the end of it. Well, it's not. Not this time! We've been through this too many times before and I'm not going to go through it again!'

She moves towards the front door of their tiny house, opens it and walks into the sitting room. Desmond follows her, closes the door with louder than usual force, and makes his way up the short flight of stairs to the bathroom. There he looks in the mirror, firstly at his injured ear, and then, holding a second mirror behind his head, looks to see what has happened there. He takes off his jumper and his shirt, both of which now have blood stains on them, and then, after washing himself down, he begins to repair the damage that Donna has inflicted.

The back of his head is sore, and he feels for but does not find any blood. However, his right ear is still bleeding. A cotton wool ball to clean it and then a couple – or three - Elastoplasts cover the damaged area quite quickly.

The bite is near his earlobe, so he will easily explain things at the dinner party tonight. An accident while he was cutting his hair – yes, he has always done his own hairdressing. 'This is the first time that the scissors have slipped in I don't know how many years.' Or a minor shaving catastrophe? Maybe that's not such a good choice as his beard works against that as an argument. Not to worry, he'll work something out. He always does.

But what to do about Donna? This time she has overstepped any kind of mark. Something will have to be done.

After coming into the house, Donna, the person who has 'overstepped the mark' has sunk into a chair, wiped her eyes and is now waiting.

Her experience is that after any show of dissent, there are repercussions. Desmond will seek revenge – not violently, he is rarely violent; he doesn't need to be. No, his revenge will be of a more insidious sort, and it may be some days or even weeks before it is exacted.

During these periods, Donna has devised a means of coping which involves her winding down her conscious state - being deliberately less sensitive to everyday activity, almost like a hibernating furry creature. So that when the act of revenge does take place, Donna is able to deal with it from within that more insulated, inured frame of mind. It's the best she can do; she can't cope in any other way.

Sitting in the chair, staring out of the window and listening to Desmond busying himself in the bathroom, she is trying to get a fix in her mind as to why she is always so helpless whenever she tries to deal with the latest challenge that he throws down in front of her.

She knows the main reason: this has never been a marriage of equals. And now, at a time when you would have thought that it didn't matter nearly so much, this inequality is now more important than it has ever been.

Donna has always been a little girl in Desmond's eyes. She was fourteen when they met, and he married her on her sixteenth birthday. When their marriage became known to Desmond's then employers, the school at which she was a pupil, he was immediately sacked - something which happened on two other occasions when new employers discovered what they called the 'unsavoury' nature of a marriage between a school employee and one of its pupils.

After their small scale, registry office wedding, Donna had immediately become a woman, a fully functioning adult. She had no adolescence, no boyfriends, no dates and no time to make romantic mistakes. Neither was there any question of her staying on at school: she was a wife - and soon, the plan went, she would be a mother. The education that she had received up until the age of sixteen was deemed by Desmond to be sufficient for her life's needs. He would be there to guide her.

The children thing did not happen. Donna never has become a mother. Her maternal instincts, such as they were, have been poured into a succession of cats and dogs, and anyway, not having children meant that they could travel more, eat out more - spend more, have a more exciting social life. And that's been a good thing, hasn't it?

While waiting for Desmond to come downstairs, these thoughts swirl around her head. Is this how it was meant to be? Coming to the final phase of their lives, desperate for money, short of friends, and without the comfort of children in their old age? No! This was the result of her first error of judgement being compounded on the next error, and the next, and so on.

Where was she in this equation? Was she truly the dutiful, believing innocent? Was there ever a time when she could have altered things? Yes, of course there was. She was responsible - at least as responsible as Desmond for allowing this impossible set of circumstances to develop.

Desmond comes downstairs, ignoring her completely. He has a huge dressing on his right ear, he must have used three or four Elastoplasts - that bite must have been a good one!

He picks up the telephone. He's calling the host - or hostess - of tonight's dinner party. He is so sorry to be such a pain, but he and Donna sadly must cry off for this evening. Donna has one of her migraines - news to Donna! - and she simply can't face going out tonight. She's curled up tight in bed fast asleep. Desmond is sorry for the really short notice, but there's nothing else he can do. No - thanks, that's very kind, but he doesn't think it right for him to come by himself. He had better stay at home and look after Donna. He is sure they will understand.

He then puts the phone down and sits looking at his wife, saying nothing, expecting her to cave in. To give up, like she always does and then ask his forgiveness. And normally, when Desmond feels that she has humiliated herself sufficiently, he will deign to welcome her back into his presence, but on condition, naturally. She will have to meet certain conditions.

He waits and waits a little longer. Donna does not respond. She is still sitting down, staring into her own private space, avoiding any eye contact, deliberately not picking up on the cues that Desmond knows he has given her.

Desmond is the first to break the silence. 'I don't like it when you criticise me.'

No response. He tries again, 'You realise how embarrassing all this is? Having to lie to our friends because of your petulance?'

Donna turns her head and sees him sitting there. He is very angry, but he is doing what he always does: letting things simmer. He has often used the phrase 'revenge is a dish best taken cold' - not with direct reference to Donna, but when talking about other slights and disappointments he has had. Maybe he is applying it to her now? Waiting for a moment to strike.

Because the situation is unusual – Donna has not 'misbehaved' like this for some time, Desmond is also unsure as to what he should do next. As they are not going out now, he toys with the thought of hurting her - just a little - but enough so that she can be reminded of how much power he retains.

In the old days - when they were much younger - Desmond quite enjoyed the various punishments that he invented. On the rare occasions that the punishment was to be physical, he obviously did not wish to leave a mark; at least, leave a mark where anyone other than he could see it. So, nipple twisting became a great favourite, and he was delighted to discover the unintended consequences that rewarded his creativity.

Donna liked it! Donna seemed to enjoy a little pain now and again, and for many years, their love life was spiced up by toys: they often used clamps, gags and paddles - there was a pair of pink fluffy handcuffs that Desmond remembers as being truly stimulating.

However, one day he went off to the shops forgetting that he had left Donna cuffed in bed, and unable to get to the bathroom. After that episode, the handcuffs disappeared.

He could easily have bought another pair, he'd picked up the last pair from a filling station as he was buying fuel, but that small event coincided with the downward spiral of his interest in her, and generally in their sexual relationship.

It's times like this that make Desmond visit what he calls his 'other side'. When he is hurt, angered or sometimes just bewildered, he must strike out, not physically, except occasionally when he gives Donna a smack. No, he prefers the secret act, the surprise, where he carefully engineers circumstances when other people feel the full force of his hatred and anger, but have no idea where it is coming from - and who is responsible for it.

Desmond's 'Mickey project' has been a great success. He wonders if Mickey has cottoned on to it yet. Mickey Hembrow, the sad little man who tries so desperately to please, the ever-willing volunteer - happy to do anything for anybody in the hope that someone acknowledges him. Mickey has been almost completely broken by Desmond and his clever ruse.

Little anonymous notes here and there, directed at Mickey and hidden where only he would find them; deliberately meant to belittle and wound him. And the masterstroke? He didn't print them or make a collage from magazine lettering - he's forged Joyce's handwriting!

Joyce Todd, 'Joyce the Mouse', that thin and weedy spinster woman who does the signs and works most Fridays, has an easy handwriting style to forge. And Desmond is a practised forger, having practised many times with, for example, Donna's signature. Joyce's signature is even easier than Donna's as she has little or no style to her writing. She has big, well-rounded lettering, ideal for price tags and shop labels, as well as for forgers.

Desmond loves to watch the way Mickey responds to the notes he sees. He collects them, quickly hiding them from others who might also see them. Desmond knows that Mickey is desperate to talk to someone about them, but who? He can see the questions in Mickey's eyes as he tries to formulate the right words to approach Desmond, but he never does. That exquisite, overwhelmingly powerful feeling that Desmond experiences each time that he looks into those sad and wounded eyes is confirmation. He is a strong man: he controls others around him. A natural leader: someone who deserves - and commands - respect.

So, wishing to use this power for good, as well as for his enjoyment as in the case of Mickey, Desmond now directs his energies differently. He has determined to build - enhance is probably the better word - his reputation in the community, and he is now focused on joining this, organising that, representing the other - and hosting memorable dinner parties, sometimes two or three a week, for their ever-increasing circle of friends and acquaintances - acquaintances, mostly. Friends seem harder to come by, but that does not stop him from trying.

This is the reason why he is so angry with Donna tonight. He was expecting that they would be breaking in to yet another new set of friends. One of the ladies at ForGiving, a recent arrival to the village, let it slip that her husband had been a diplomat, an ambassador no less, and that their retirement to the Lakes had followed a very successful career.

Desmond had quickly managed to insinuate himself into a new friendship with this lady, so much so that she had asked him if he and Donna would care to join them for a bite of supper.

He had leapt at the invitation and had already worked out how he would impress his newly-found diplomatic friend with examples of his own successes.

An ambassador! And Donna was playing the spoiled child again.

He can't resist doing something to put Donna in her place - he won't leave things like they are as she mustn't be allowed to win - ever! So, moving quickly towards her, he gives her a swift hair pull with a long twist, holding her head and bringing her face very close to his - before shoving her away to land in a heap back on the sofa.

That's enough - for now. He's still the boss - and she needs to remember that. He might revisit the scene later, but now, seeing that they are not to be dining with new friends tonight, Desmond will reward himself, and he knows exactly what form that reward will take.

He pours himself a large whisky. He enjoys whisky and keeps an impressive selection of single malts - mostly to impress his guests - but for his own enjoyment too on occasions like this.

He thinks back to when he was a child, maybe when he was about ten years old. That first black and white television they had at home often would show films where 'Father' would come home at the end of a hard day at the office. A stiff whisky before dinner - measured in fingers 'two or three fingers', seemed perfectly normal. And so, it is in Desmond's household - gin and tonic is for relaxing in company, whisky is therapeutic and best enjoyed alone.

He measures himself three fingers of a peaty malt, Ardbeg tonight, one of the Islay malts that he truly enjoys. This will be a special time, this evening - yes, he deserves it - and this might be the first of several whiskies he will enjoy tonight.

He retreats to the little downstairs room that he calls his 'den', and he fires up his computer. Donna will not disturb him there: she knows the price that she would pay if she did. He waits patiently to engage with his own private vice - something he does three or four times a week if he has the chance. No, not porn, pornography doesn't interest him at all - no, his guilty secret is to be found in the vortex of the roulette wheel, a game that now has captured his entire being. He logs in to his account and the young lady on the computer says, 'Hello Desmond, welcome back' to him. Yes, she is an avatar, but her friendly smile draws him further in. He is at home here.

Tonight, he is in credit by a little over two hundred pounds, the result of a small win last night. He plunges in headfirst with a one-hundred-pound bet on black. The wheel spins and the little white ball lands on red.

Bollocks! Try again! He takes a long pull of his drink as that beguiling wheel comes back into view on the screen. Another hundred pounds on black and again, it lands on red. Maybe it's the round figure, the hundred. If he were to bet say, ninety-nine pounds, maybe that would change his luck? That would mean going into a loss tonight, but this is an investment, isn't it?

He's gone too far now, so he must carry on. He's had a little luck recently, so it's not all bad news, and he is sure that he'll be able to recoup his losses. He takes another sip of his whisky as works out his next bet. He wagers another hundred pounds, but this time on four different numbers. The wheel spins again, and Desmond crosses his fingers. See if that works!

All in all, he's over seventeen thousand pounds down: that total is split between his and Donna's now depleted savings account and the ForGiving takings that he has been appropriating.

The saving grace has been his personal accounting system at ForGiving. It's fool proof - so far. On the evenings that he closes the shop - about four times a week, he re-enters each transaction of the day on to a new till roll, reducing the cash turnover, by deleting the more expensive items paid for by cash, by approximately twenty five percent. He pockets the excess cash and destroys the original till roll. That is the money that goes into his roulette fund - and day-to-day expenses.

He knows that his roulette system is a perfect choice, and he believes completely - particularly when bolstered with the confidence of a couple of large whiskies - that this challenge of the seventeen thousand pounds will soon simply disappear.

That twenty-six pounds that the till was up tonight will find its way on to his cash card on Monday, making a total of over two hundred and fifty pounds gleaned from last week, less than he would have wished, but nothing big was sold.

Seeking to reconcile the till is a charade that he conducts with Donna and with any other person who sits next to him as he cashes up each night. It is something that he has always kept from Donna and it is important, because now he needs to be able to continue his mission to get his money back. This money will enable him to buy some extra credit - not that he will need it; there's a sense of optimism in the air tonight.

And he can do it: he knows his chance is about to happen. The big win, the one that will solve all his problems. He has even thought what he will do with his winnings. When the big win arrives, and after he clears his debts, he plans to make a big donation to ForGiving as his goodbye present to the charity.

There will be an official thank you, obviously, and all the people with whom he has worked over the last few years will see this altruism and amazing generosity as a sign of his substance as a man - somebody to be reckoned with. Not many charity shop managers make a large donation to their charity when they retire, and this will make him stand out, no doubt about that, no doubt at all.

His numbers don't come up - again! Only two weeks ago, he was two thousand pounds ahead and on a run. True, his luck has changed, but it can change at any time. He tells himself: 'Play the system - play the system! Don't go off piste again!' That was the big mistake. His system worked well - and was successful - two thousand pounds in two days! Then he started to be clever - too clever - and the losses began.

Another whisky is called for - serious thinking requires serious drinking! He fills his glass and while he is up, he goes into the living room. Donna has not moved. She looks at him sullenly and quietly says, 'I hate you.'

'I know, Dee, but you never learn. I have to keep you in check, otherwise you misbehave.'

'You don't get it, do you? I'm not the child here. You are! I have been looking after you for years! And the genuinely sad thing is that I am likely to have to do it again.'

'Meaning?'

'You are flouncing out of yet another job.'

'I'm not flouncing out of anything. This is a considered decision.'

Donna is not giving up this time. 'If it's as considered as most of your other decisions, we're up the creek again!'

'Up the creek? You become more stupid by the minute. I don't know why I still put up with you.'

He lifts his glass - another three fingers - toasts Donna without saying anything to her, and returns to his computer, closing the door behind him. He'll show them. Roulette - and that attractive croupier - will be the answer- so let it spin! And spin it does.

In the sitting room, the tears have started. Donna decides to make herself a cup of tea and go to bed. She's lost faith in this man; she can't believe in him, so it no longer matters to her if he crashes and burns - again.

Circumstances now are different from previous occasions. In the past, with dead businesses, unhappy employers and suspicious colleagues, Donna has also suffered all the guilt and the soul-searching that accompanied each episode. Sometimes that guilt has required a quick escape: a midnight flit leaving unpaid debts and outstanding rent is not unknown to them. But no longer. She's not going down that route anymore. She feels at home here, more at home than she has ever felt. But Desmond and her?

It's broken; can't be fixed, and she no longer intends to be part of this train crash of a life. She made a huge mistake, but that was so long ago as to be completely irrelevant. She should have left him, but now it's too late - 'sell-by date' and all that.

There is the hint of a possibility of her escaping, something on the horizon should she choose to take it, but more than likely she will have to stick around and put up with whatever follows. She decides that from now on, she will not worry herself or be emotionally engaged the next time Desmond comes to grief. In her heart, she knows that that she can't be this dispassionate, but she is going to try.

***

It's not been a good weekend for Desmond on many levels, and when he comes in to open ForGiving on Monday, he arrives alone - Donna, still refusing to talk to him, never mind come in to the shop.

The old methods haven't worked; try as he may, he could not bend her round to his way of thinking. She simply wouldn't budge!

Even when he said that ok, he wouldn't walk out of the ForGiving job, she simply said that she didn't believe him. To be fair to her, she had a point, but nevertheless, he had expected her to come to the surface by now. This has been the longest period of insubordination that Desmond has ever experienced in his marriage. He doesn't like it but must admit to himself that he has no idea what to do about it.

And his roulette evening was a disaster! So much for his system - he was wiped out! He's thinking about what went wrong as he drives to the shop. All that research! All the effort that he had put in - not to devising his own system - that would be stupid, but to choosing the best system available on the internet.

He had been carefully through the intricacies of well over twenty internet gambling systems before investing fifty dollars in one that was guaranteed to work - 'or your money back'. He's not entirely sure that he's going to get his money back, but he will try - once he can get a grip on the present situation - a 'no money' present situation.

His credit cards are all maxed out - he has twenty odd pounds hanging around from Saturday's till receipts, and that is all. He was relieved to find that his car had half a tank of fuel in it. That at least means that he can get to and from home for a while.

The day-to-day bills, the direct debits and the standing orders might be ok for a little longer, but they will soon start to bounce unless he can get some money into the bank account - and quickly! He can't think of an answer; this is almost a first for him. He has extricated himself out of many a mess in his time, but what to do here?

And he's lost Donna! She's determined - at least she says she is - to have nothing to do with him. No halving of the problem by sharing it this time. She has always been there before, always there to blame when one of his projects has gone tits up. This is all his doing; he can't even retrieve some self-respect by turning it into her fault - she has no idea of what has been going on.

In one sense, he has been saving her from reality. He can allow himself some kudos there. He has kept her insulated from the truth of their situation. They have been living a life way beyond their financial ability to sustain it, and he has kept that knowledge away from his wife. That was doing her a favour, wasn't it?

The harder they have tried, the less successful they have been in being recognised and valued. Desmond is a man of the world, he is a traveller - never a tourist, exactly like one of the other volunteers, Monica. He remembers her using that phrase, and he thought that it was so apt, and applied to him perfectly.

Donna always looks and dresses the part to perfection, but somehow, it doesn't seem to click. People are polite, normally, but Desmond and Donna are seldom invited back - no matter how many invitations of theirs are taken up by their many new acquaintances.

So, this is their nadir, as low as it gets. Broke, with him about to walk out of another job, a lousy job, granted, but knowing that the chances of getting another, any other, are less than slim. And Donna? She seems to be in a dark place.   For the first time ever in what has been their decades-long relationship, Desmond can see her walking out on him. If only she had somewhere to go. She hasn't; he has seen to that.   That might be the saving grace.

He arrives at ForGiving and the first person he sees is Joyce Todd, a little wispy lady who usually works on a Friday.

'Hi Joyce! Mondays? Is somebody ill?'

Joyce looks nervous. 'I wanted to have a word with you, so I thought that I'd come before people start to arrive. I hope that's ok.'

'It's fine. Happy to see you. We don't see each other often enough - what with you coming in on a Friday. It's a bad day for Donna and me - banking, reports. In fact, I'm thinking about getting rid of Fridays altogether - I don't think that Friday does anybody any good at all.'

He's smiling, but notices that Joyce has not picked up on the humour. 'It was a joke, Joyce. I suppose a lot of people like Fridays. But I will have my way with November!'

'What do you mean?'

'November? It's a dreadful month. Weather - it's boring - nothing happens, apart from the moustaches. I'd ban it. Do away with it altogether. That's if I was king of the world. What do you think?'

'My birthday's in November.'

'In that case, Joyce, I'll focus my attention on February. When I am king of the world, your birthday will be safe with me - and all those middle managers can continue to grow their moustaches. Now what did you want to see me about? Can I as the king of ...?'

'It's rather delicate.' The tone of her interjection stamps on the atmosphere of levity that Desmond has tried to inject into the conversation. 'I wasn't sure if I should come and see you at all.'

'Why?' Desmond's riff has come to an end as he sees that there is something troubling in those little eyes of the sixty-odd-year-old spinster. She doesn't do jokes, that's for sure, but there is an edginess that Desmond has not seen before.

He takes her into the back room and finds a chair for her. Then he sits down and looks at her. He smiles and says, 'OK, Joyce. You have my full attention. How can I help you?'

She takes the seat, and clutching her handbag tightly, she says, 'I believe that someone is stealing from ForGiving.'

'Stealing?' First response from Desmond - about as much as he can muster at this point. Is his face blooming? Are rivulets of sweat making him look like the guilty thief he is? Probably not, but his heartbeat has certainly gone up a notch or two, and he is finding that it is rather more difficult to breathe than normally is the case.

And his mouth has gone dry! When he decides to continue with his questioning, he finds that the words have stuck in his throat. He has to cough, gently, just to free them.

'What makes you think that somebody has been stealing, Joyce? This is a charity. People don't steal from charities. We have the occasional shoplifter, is that what you mean?'

Joyce snorts derisively, at least that is evidently her intention. She is not made for derisive snorting, so it doesn't work too well. Joyce is small, bird like and very shy. Her natural demeanour is one of dignified anonymity, and she is desperately hoping to revert to this her normal state as soon as she can. She is obviously uncomfortable but decides to plough on.

'No. I mean stealing. In that I believe that much of what we sell, much of the money that we make, is being stolen on a regular basis. I propose to inform the police and I wanted to let you know.'

'Thank you for the courtesy, Joyce. This is a serious accusation. May I ask, are you accusing anybody in particular of this - me for example?'

'I don't know if it is you,' Joyce replies. 'It could be you, I suppose. You are one of the obvious possibilities, so I certainly can't rule you out. But as you have devolved much of the responsibility for day-to-day organisation to other people, and I only come in on a Friday, I would want to be sure before I accused anyone, including you.'

Desmond sees a chink of light here. Not much of one, but definitely a chink.

'If you are not sure,' he is hoping to head her off at the pass.

'Oh, I am sure. I am absolutely sure. I don't know if the thief is you or somebody else. But I do have proof that there is a thief here at ForGiving.'

You've heard the saying, 'his bowels turned to water'? Desmond has never experienced that feeling before - he does now!

'You say you have proof, Joyce? How can you have proof? You only come in for one half day a week.'

'True, but I have a system, and I have been following it for over three months now. My system proves that money is being taken from the till. I don't quite know how the thief does it - maybe by falsifying till returns - that would seem the obvious way, but my system...'

Desmond interrupts her, 'You say that you have proof. A system? Proof would be important if you are going to take these allegations further.'

'I will take them as far as I need to take them. Be assured of that. I have come to see you out of a courtesy. If you are the thief, you need to know what I am going to do. I am not a vindictive person, I simply want the thefts to stop - and the thief punished, of course,' she adds almost as an afterthought.

She continues, 'Do you think that people who steal from charities have a special kind of flaw in their character? I do. More sad than evil. So, stopping the theft, maybe catching the person too - that would be good - but stopping the theft is what I mainly want to happen.'

'So, tell me about your system, Joyce. You see, I'm not convinced that there has been anything stolen - not along the lines that you suggest. I need - we would need - more in the way of certainty - evidence. If I can't agree with your suspicions, I think that we'll have difficulty in getting anybody else to pursue this.'

Joyce looks at Desmond and then opens the clasp of her old lady's handbag, a handbag that has a strong gold-looking bar along the top of it, with a clasp comprising two little balls that need to be forced past each other for the bag to open.

'Here you are,' she says. 'This is my system.' Desmond is now looking at dozens and dozens of price tags, tags of the kind that Joyce and the others place on items as they come into the shop.

'On my Friday shift, I create a second tag for each item that I see with a price of more than eight pounds. Eight pounds was a random choice, but I assumed that the thief would want to maximise his or her return.'

'Maximise their return? A bit technical, don't you think?'

'Look at me, Desmond. No, look at me, please. What do you see? You don't need to answer because I know.' She smiles, 'The answer is nothing. I don't appear on your radar - nor on the radar of anybody else. Nice, anonymous Joyce, that's me.

'And that's how I wanted it to remain. I came up to the Lakes to retire, to enjoy a more relaxed lifestyle. And I work at ForGiving because I truly appreciate altruism - it's the most beautiful of all human qualities. Altruism is important to me, part of my personal philosophy you might say, because it has filled a void in my own life. I have never been able to enjoy close relationships - maybe because I am such a mouse, but I appreciate the good in other people. And there is good here. The people who work here are wonderful, and they have lifted my spirit - until I found that there was a thief who is undermining it all.'

'Joyce, you have shown me some price tags. Nothing else!'

'Before I came here, for over twenty years I worked as a floor walker, a shop detective for a big department store in Liverpool. That was then, and this is now, and I sincerely did not want to get involved with that kind of game again, but then, this happened!' And she points to the price tags that can be seen in her handbag.

'I am trying to assume that you have not noticed this criminal behaviour, Desmond. And if that is the case, I'll simply conclude that you are incompetent as a manager!' She sees Desmond ruffle his feathers and says, 'Wait a minute, please. It gets worse.'

Desmond, who was going to try to pass this event off as the rantings of an old biddy, is now trying to marshal his thoughts differently.

'And if you do know about these thefts - or did know - you are more than incompetent, you are stupid! This is the oldest trick in the book. Look here.'

She takes out five or six price tags. All have the bar code on them which allows for items, once processed, to be scanned into the till.

'Each of these is an item which I duplicated, and although they have all been sold - at least, they are no longer anywhere in the shop - they don't appear on any till roll.'

'You have checked?'

'Of course, I have checked! I have been used to catching fraud in a daily turnover of thousands of pounds. Here, we do a couple of hundred, if we are lucky. This was easy – easier than a training exercise.

'We take the tags off the clothes as we sell them. The tags give us an idea of our stock levels, and they act as a way of reconciling. If we had a computerised point-of-sale system, this fiddle would no longer be possible, but as we don't, we leave this area to the honesty of the people involved. And this being a charity …'

As the words tail off, Desmond has no idea how to respond: Joyce, however, has.

'Are you the thief, Desmond?'

'Me? Joyce! How could you? No! Of course, I am not the thief.' He is getting his bearings now; the situation is not as bad as it might be. If she had absolute proof, she could have come out and accused him directly.

'I've come to see you this morning because I want to give you the chance - if you are the thief - to make things right. I've said I am not a vindictive person, and I truly believe that anyone who steals from a shop like ours must be sick, rather than evil - or desperate.

'So, if there are pressures on you - stresses - that have caused you to behave out of character, I think that I would understand that. All I request is that you pay back the money. I've got three months' data here, and we could extrapolate a figure from that for the year. If you were the thief - and if you were thinking of paying the money back, I calculate that over the last three months, you would have stolen about fifteen hundred pounds.'

And she is spot on! Sixteen hundred and fifty, to be more exact, but who's counting - oh yes, she is counting.

'Joyce, I'm not the thief, and I don't know what else to say! If this is true, it's terrible!' Desmond has decided: he will wing it. 'I want to thank you for all this work - you have done a wonderful job. If you wish to leave it in my hands…'

'You know what I'm going to say to that, don't you? I can't! Nothing personal, but the best way forward - if you are not the thief and so you are not going to pay the money back - the best way forward is for us to send the evidence to the regional office at ForGiving. And we'll also inform the police. Then we should leave it up to them to decide what to do. We don't want to be involved in any investigation, as we are both too close to it in so many ways.'

'You think that we have lost fifteen hundred pounds during the last three months?'

'Yes, I do. The tags mount up to more than that, but I want to be realistic. There is no record of any of these tags being accounted for. Over a full year, that would be over six thousand pounds, and that is a lot of money to go missing. That's the situation; what do you think we should do?'

Is this Desmond's chance? Does she want him to decide the next steps? He attempts to take the initiative.

'I need to think about this, Joyce. This is worrying - and we need to catch whoever is responsible.'

'Why did you not know about it?' She's a terrier, this woman.

'I'm not saying that. I had my suspicions, but I don't have your - expertise. You'll know that I have never been involved in retail sales before, I worked in schools until I retired. You have done the kind of work that I should have been doing, and I need to look at your evidence and work out where we go from here.'

Joyce is not convinced. 'Too late for that. This is something that you should have been doing already. I came to see you first, because you have the chance to put things right.'

The balance has shifted again, and Desmond senses it. 'I have the chance?'

'Of course! Desmond, we are being too British about this. You are the thief and we both know it. There is nobody else who could remove the tags and steal all this money. It is you.'

'Wait a minute!'

'And you disabled the time stamp facility on the till!'

'I have done nothing of the sort!'

'Sorry Desmond, no more prevarication! That was my first clue, don't you see? It's possibly something that the other volunteers wouldn't pick up on, but both you and I know that you can use that till to stamp each purchase with both the date and the time of sale. That would have made your scam so much more difficult, so you disabled it. A very risky thing for you to do, and I am amazed that the regional manager hasn't picked up on it.'

Is this what a heart attack feels like? Desmond's chest is constricted, it's so tight - he is finding it difficult to breathe. He wants to deal with Joyce, to find the Ace to her King, but he knows he can't. She has got him: she has worked it all out - and he thought that he'd a fool-proof method working for him.

'What are you going to do?' He needs to get a bottom line here, so he asks her. When he knows what Joyce has in mind, he thinks that possibly, just possibly, he might be able to swerve this. How and when he is not sure, but he needs to know her intentions first.

'I want you to know that I am disappointed, that's the first thing. I had hoped that it wasn't you, but I think that we both know that the police will be able to work it out. But I do have a question.'

'A question? What?'

'How did you get around the audit? The auditors should have picked up on this. They should have seen that the till had been re-programmed, apart from anything else - they have been very remiss.'

This is the moment. This is Desmond's one opportunity. He will throw himself at her mercy. If he were to explain how difficult his financial situation is, she will understand, won't she?

Too late! Joyce has stood up. She's put all the tags back in her handbag and snapped it closed.

'I'm leaving the shop before anyone else comes in; I don't want to embarrass you any further. This is what I propose. You have until the end of the week to replace the money that you have stolen - shall we say six thousand? I'm sure that this has been going on for longer than that, but I can't prove it. If you are able to replace it, I don't know how you will explain the sudden influx of money, but I don't care. What I want to see is ForGiving doing what it is supposed to do - giving help to people who need it, not providing you with your very own piggy bank.

'You will have to resign, and I imagine that ForGiving will prosecute you, and that is a risk you'll have to take. You have until Friday to straighten things out; after that I'm going to the police.'

Desmond is still: no movement at all – banjaxed, poleaxed, completely flattened. She continues, 'I don't know if you expected some kind of easy way out - maybe you did. But you are a thief, Desmond. You don't deserve an easy way out. You have been stealing from a charity shop. It's difficult to forgive that - very difficult to forgive that.'

She stands up to go. Desmond moves in front of her, preventing her from leaving, 'Joyce, this will ruin me, you know that. Can't you see some way...?'

'You are ruined already, Desmond, and you must have been for some time. This - your deciding to steal from ForGiving didn't ruin you. I didn't ruin you. I discovered what had been happening, that's all. This is all self-inflicted - and you will get what you deserve.

'And let me explain why I am so disappointed. I discovered the Lakes many years ago when my store bought an old hotel here in Ambleton. They bought it for their staff, and I was one of the first people to come. Ever since then, I took almost all my holidays in the Lakes, and I was able to move here when I retired. My memories are almost all happy ones, but now you have polluted them. Friday - you have until Friday!'

And she leaves. This tiny, mouse-like woman bows her head, looks to the floor and reverts to the passive, invisible presence that until now, has always been Joyce.

***

There's another surprise waiting for Desmond when he arrives home. He's in a foul mood already, his mind awash with all the various escape routes that he might attempt. He's searching the combinations that may or may not work to help extricate him from the Joyce dilemma.

But so far, no luck. As far as he can tell, his goose is fully cooked. And now there is Donna to face.

This morning she didn't even say goodbye to him. He asked her if she was coming into ForGiving - and she yawned! That was a no, evidently, as she then turned over in bed and pretended to go back to sleep.

He's expecting more of the same as he gets out of his car and goes into the house, and here is where the surprise comes in.

'Hi!' says Donna, smiling. Smiling! 'I should have been with you today, sorry!'

This mood swing is most unlike Donna. Once she descends into what he refers to as 'toxic' mode, Donna can be impossible for weeks, but now, surprisingly, she seems to have brightened up.

'I've been baking and cooking all day. Open the wine and we'll have a glass before dinner. And you can tell me what you have been up to at the shop.'

So, it appears that he has died and is now in heaven. Desmond is bemused. 'What's happened? You were furious with me all weekend, and now you're all smiles.'

'I got over myself.'

'How did you do that?'

'Some serious introspection. I have been online - looking around for something to cheer me up. I was unhappy, so I thought that I would see if there was anything I could do -apart from poisoning your food. That was a joke, by the way.

'I went on to some self-help websites. I found one which was talking about anger - and about being angry. That's me, I thought. 'Mrs Angry'.

'It was fascinating - and it made me think. It went on a bit about how anger is generated, but then the guy said something that I thought was very interesting. He said that my anger is not your fault, and I should not be blaming you.'

'Really?'

'Not exactly - it is your bloody fault, and we both know that! Let me get this right. It said that I have a right to be angry - if I feel that I am justified in that anger. And I am - I think that we could both conclude that, don't you?'

'And if I do conclude that?' Desmond is still not sure about where this is going.

'Thinking 'angry' is one thing - and that is what I have the right to do. My feelings are primal, and that kind of anger must come out. And it makes me want to explode.

'It's what I do with those feelings that matters. It works in stages. The first stage is when I 'feel' the anger. They tell me to feel no guilt there at all, and I am ok with that.

'The next stage is thinking about those feelings, and the third stage is expressing them through my behaviours. How I choose to express my anger is critical. Are you with me so far?'

'In a way, yes. In another way, I can't follow you at all. I am confused. Are you angry with me or not angry with me?' In truth, Desmond is delighted. He was expecting the 'toxic witch' Donna that he had left in bed this morning - now he is talking to Mother Theresa.

She continues with her theme: ''Behaving' angry is something else. Do you see? Those angry strops, my refusal to talk to you - and my genuine wish to throw you out of the window? You don't make me angry - I make me angry! I have chosen to be angry. I can choose to behave differently, and I have. This makes sense to me now, and I have started to work with it.'

'You are still angry, though?'

'Yes, livid, but in a more refined way!' She smiles and takes a sip of her wine.

'I like this kind of anger,' Desmond says. 'I hope that you are comfortable with it.'

And he smiles back at his extremely weird wife. He is assuming that she has been slightly hypnotised by some psychobabble, although a little part of him wonders if she has tipped herself over the edge.

Surprisingly, the evening that Desmond had so dreaded passes in a pleasantly civilised way. Always a good cook, Donna has excelled herself tonight, and together, the two of them enjoy a beautifully prepared meal. Their conversation is polite - a little guarded, but polite - so polite that later, after they have both enjoyed an extra couple of glasses of wine, Desmond decides to broach the subject of Joyce, or at least, as much of that topic that he can divulge safely.

'Joyce Todd came to see me this morning.'

'Joyce the Mouse?' They have always referred to Joyce that way. 'What did she squeak?' Donna thinks that she has cracked a terrific joke and collapses into a fit of giggles.

The pity for Desmond is that he has yet to explain the Joyce thing. Otherwise he would have been in there! Getting Donna to laugh like that is virtually a free ticket to getting her into bed.

Granted, that's not quite as exciting a prospect as it used to be, but an amenable Donna is going to be of much more value to him than the harridan that he was dreading as he drove home.

'Yes, she wanted to see me about something important - something that she thought was important, anyway.'

'And it was?'

'Probably not. She thinks that somebody has been removing things from the shop. Stuff that hasn't been paid for has disappeared.'

'She knows that I take clothes home to try on. Doesn't everyone?'

'A bit more serious than that.'

'Like what?'

'She seems to think that someone is removing valuable items, and not paying for them.'

'I always return the things I don't want. Again, doesn't everyone?'

Desmond emphasises the one point he needs to make, 'I think that she is talking about me, not you. And not about clothes - she has the idea that I may be' - he searches for the form of words, 'that I might be operating some kind of fiddle - a scam.'

'And are you?'

'Of course not! She has a bee in her bonnet, that's all.'

'Well, I hope that she gets stung by it; that's all I have to say on the matter.'

Should he let it go? Should he press home a little further? He decides to walk the tightrope.

'She suggested that I might be the person doing it.   Naturally, I was outraged, and I let her know how disappointed I was. But you won't be able to use the ForGiving van for a while - I think that is what it is truly about. I am guessing here, but I would not be surprised if that was it.'

'The ForGiving van?'

'Yes, she's always moaning about that. She thinks that people misuse it.'

The ForGiving van is an old Ford Transit van that somebody had donated to the shop. Desmond had had it made legal, and it was now used to transport goods, make the occasional delivery and so on.

'She thought its use was being abused. Those were her words exactly. I - you and I probably use it more than anybody, so she's come and had a go at me.

'And she also talked about some money going missing, but I think that I was able to straighten her out there.'

Donna thinks about Joyce the Mouse for a moment. 'But Joyce is such a shy little thing! I am surprised that she said anything at all. She never volunteers any opinion. Are you sure? I mean, could you be mistaken?'

'No. I'm not mistaken - and she says that she can prove her suspicions.'

'Did she tell you how?'

Here, Desmond takes a step backwards - a difficult manoeuvre on the tightrope on which he is now balanced. He wants to be careful about how much information he shares with Donna. She might find it difficult to deal with the truth. After all, he is struggling with it himself, and he knows everything.

'No,' he replies. 'She said that she intends to go to the police at the end of the week. She is not sure if I am involved - again, her words - but she has enough information to prove that something is going wrong. It's not only the van: money is going missing, and she wants to inform ForGiving head office and the police, so that they will be able to get to the bottom of it.'

'Why doesn't she go straight to the police?'

'Here's the interesting bit. She says that she wants the charity to get its money back. She's not too concerned about the fiddles - just that if the charity is losing money, she sees that as unfair, and wants it resolved.'

'Resolved?'

'Yes, she wants the money put back.'

'How much?'

'She didn't say. I told her that I would look into it and see if there is anything - amiss. I don't think there is, but I will show her some of my evidence, and that will diffuse the situation.'

'Is it you? Is that why she came to see you? Have you been taking money from ForGiving?' Donna goes right to the heart of the issue.

'Donna! What are you saying? Don't be ridiculous!'

'If you have, and if she has evidence, we are in deep trouble.'

'I haven't! And we are not! I will fix this. She seems to have latched on to some - minor issue - something tiny and insignificant, and she has magnified it in her imagination. Remember, she has nothing going on in her life, so tiny things take on a great importance.'

'Thank you, Dr Freud! What a pathetic response! We could be in trouble here - and you know it!'

'How? Because some silly old woman has become obsessed...'

'Because there's probably some truth in it!'

Desmond can't hide his surprise. He thought that he was playing the innocent victim very well, but obviously not.

Donna continues, 'I know you well enough - too well, frankly. And I know you are lying. You are involved in something - unsavoury, and I am guessing that Joyce is probably right. You are desperately trying to work things out - but you are fighting on two fronts.'

'Meaning?'

'It's your phrase - you know exactly what it means. Joyce has worried you - she seriously has you worried. But you are more worried about me. I suspect - my suspicion, not Joyce's, is that you have sanitised the conversation you had with her for my benefit. It's much more serious than you are pretending, otherwise you wouldn't have said anything at all.'

'That's not true!'

'And while you are fighting this on two fronts - mine and Joyce's - you are going to lose! So, Desmond, let's have it. This time it's important. Let me know what is going on - now!'

And he does. A complete capitulation - well, almost! He tells Donna about the scam, how it works, and how it has kept them afloat for - well, forever. The money that he has taken from ForGiving has supplemented their income, and it's that money that's kept their heads above water.

He doesn't mention the roulette. He thinks about it but decides that enough is enough.

'And is that everything?' comes Donna's timely question. He replies that yes, that is everything. By that, he means that it is everything for now. He has no idea how - or indeed, if - he is going to explain the gambling, or how he has frittered away the small amount of money that they had been able to put to one side.

'Anyway, I do feel that we should be moving on. Let's get away from here - new horizons. Monica is itching to take over. It would be a good time for both of us, and we talked about this on Saturday, remember?'

He is aware that they are both a bit elderly for a flit, but with a bit of teeing up, he is now sure that Donna could well be up for it too.

Also, he's certain that his luck is due to change and tonight, back at the magic spinning wheel of fortune, everything will have turned around. He'll be back in credit with his bank - he can feel it in his water.

The Joyce scenario, and this current financial embarrassment is nothing new to Desmond. It's a little more critical than most of his escapades have been, but he has lived all his life on that cusp, one step away from potential disaster. Each business venture that fell to its death was accompanied by similar challenges - and he remembers them all too well.

It's likely that they will have to prepare for a sharp exit, and quickly. They'll miss Ambleton and the Lakes after living here all these years, and the chances are that even his wizard-like powers may not entirely extricate them this time.

That little *gite* in France that they often visit has a certain allure. He is sure that he could get a job there. Maybe a tour guide? Maybe teaching English as a foreign language? He is optimistic that if they do manage to get away - and quickly, they'll be able to pick up the pieces.

What he does need to do is placate Donna, so that she is on his side, and then his native wit and cunning will see them through. This will be his strategy.

'I'm so sorry for the mess. I didn't know what else to do.'

'Forgive me for stating the obvious, but why didn't you let me know?'

'Let you know what? I hoped that I could get things back together without worrying you. I was thinking of you all the time.'

Donna gives this outrageous lie the value it deserves.   'That's balls! If you are going to continue treating me as an idiot, I warn you, I'll leave you to rot!'

'I'm not treating you as an idiot ...'

'If my instincts are right, you are probably leaving out the criminal, the really serious stuff.' She looks at him, sees him flinch, 'Thought so!'

'But that's up to you. I can help you - I am probably the only person who can - but only because I don't want to be tarred with this brush. I don't yet know how, but I know that it would be better for you to work with me than against me.

'On the other hand, if you continue to patronise me - condescend to me - any more, I am going to leave you.'

'What?'

'You heard.'

Desmond pulls out the last arrow from his quiver, 'And where will you go?' This arrow has always struck home in the past.

'Let me worry about that - oh, and let me tell you to worry about it as well. I'm no longer the china doll wife. I'm not a pet, not a child - not an idiot any more. You have overstepped once too often, and this is what I will do.

'Unless we sort this properly, I'm leaving you. I know where I am going, and I know who I am going with.'

Going with? Desmond tries to interject, not with words, but he looks so startled by what she has just said, and that is a question in itself.

'I like you, Desmond. I love you, always have.' Desmond can feel a 'but' coming here. And it does.

'But don't even ask! All you need to know I is that I am no longer dependent on you, unless I choose to be. However, I also don't want to be shamed by you; I have a life to live, even if it turns out that you don't, and that is why I want us to fix this thing - properly.'

'I think we will have to go to France, Donna.'

'France? Don't you think they'll find us there straight away?'

'France to begin with - then who knows?'

It seems that the balance has tilted. The unthinkable thought - getting away from here, with Donna's consent, has quickly become a possibility.

France for starters. It's true that they would be found very quickly if they went down to their little *gite* in France. But further afield? Romania? Bulgaria? Desmond's mind is working overtime. How much cash can he lay his hands on? Their credit cards are useless, but if they were to flit - a few days to make sure they've packed enough, and maybe borrowing some cash from someone, anyone.

Desmond has a Post Office Money card. He can put cash on it whenever he wants and build up a balance - but laying his hands on enough of it is going to be the real challenge.

This is a very implausible plan; he's aware of this, but apart from robbing a bank, he can't think of anything else.

It's good to know that Donna is still on his side. And they do have until Friday to sort all this out before Joyce wreaks her havoc.

* * *

Donna is in a quandary too. She has choices that she can make. She wasn't bluffing when she told Desmond that she would leave him. She has options, and now, with what she believes is likely to happen, she might have to exercise one of them.

Her 'options' are both men, both widowers and both solvent. That's the good news, particularly the 'solvent' part. That would be a new experience.

In his own unique way, and slowly over a period of months, each of these gentlemen has come on to Donna and, quietly and oh, so politely, offered her an alternative to continuing to live with Desmond. They have both made a regular habit out of popping in to the ForGiving shop and engaging Donna in conversation - although never on the same day or at the same time as their rival.

They are aware that they are in competition, so to speak, and Donna has been equally considerate to each of her swains, neither offering too much in the way of encouragement, nor dismissing their protestations of love with disdain. She has always been a bit of a flirt and has always loved attention from men - even if the men concerned are more than slightly foxed, as in this case.

Given how difficult it has been on occasion, Desmond always being around and the shop constantly full of people, it is a tribute to both old boys how they have each managed to indicate their wishes, their best-case scenario - and in each best case offered, it will involve Donna dumping Desmond and moving in with one of them.

Of course, there is also bad news. Option One is in his late seventies, maybe even older. He is lonely and smells a little too much of many years of neglect. He wants a nurse, that's all, and in thinking about his offer, Donna did reflect on whether she might get as much fun out of that idea as she had a few years ago when her sexy nurse's outfit proved so popular with Desmond. Her reluctant conclusion is sadly not. Option One is an old man and he wants a real nurse.

But Donna is still young: she still has it - as evidenced by her two suitors - and the next few years are going to be important to her. These years must not become defined by ill-fitting false teeth and unpleasant smells.

She'll keep Option One on the back burner; however, it would be a pity if he popped off and she were to find that there was a great pile of money with her name on it - now going to some long-vanished relative! Should she ask him for something upfront, a financial consideration, a monetary token of his regard? She will think that one through.

Option Two is much more promising, attractive even. Recently widowed a couple of years ago, Option Two sold his three shops in Blackpool after his wife's death and moved to a pleasant bungalow in the Lakes, close to Ambleton.

He's told Donna that he's joined the Masons and that he plays bowls occasionally. During one of their brief conversations in ForGiving, he also confided to Donna that she was his 'ideal woman', and he would relish, truly relish, the opportunity of making her every wish come true.

Donna's heart skipped a little beat at that thought, although the Masons and the bowls club don't suggest that Option Two will be the international playboy that would be her next 'Desmond of choice'. But he's younger than she is and not bad looking, so there might be a chance of rekindling some embers. If she must choose one of her options, this will be it - although she would be still interested in getting Option One to put his money where his mouth is - along with those ill-fitting dentures.

Desmond knows nothing of this, and Donna does not propose to rock his already unsteady boat - yet. Let's see what the master plan is, she thinks - and then I'll blow it up. The truth? Donna is staying where she is - here in the Lakes. She's no intention of being chased around Europe - maybe if she was with a thirty-year-old stud, she might consider it - for a few weeks at least. But with Desmond, and his prostate problems? No thank you!

Option Two looks to be the favourite! You can learn to love bowls, can't you?

***

It's now Thursday and Desmond has spent all week trying to get some money together. His Post Office Money card has six hundred and fifteen pounds on it. That's all that he has been able to scrape together, so first-class travel is probably out. So is any other kind of travel.

He and Donna have hit upon a plan. They will go to see Joyce. If they can get Joyce to change her mind, to give them a little more time, they will be able to plan for a more graceful exit than the fraught-with-danger fast escape that seems to be their only current possibility.

'What will we say to her?' Desmond is concerned. He's no idea what the pretext might be for their visit to Joyce. Neither of them has been to Joyce's house before. But it is right in the middle of Ambleton, so they will be able to walk round there if they park next to Alfred Hitchcock's, the town's cinema and restaurant complex.

It's still light as Desmond parks across the road from the cinema, and he's already worrying that he might be seen going to Joyce's. She lives in a small, terraced house between Alfred's and Bold Street, and they've decided that it would be better not to park too close.

Sitting around at home, it's been a long wait, and a nervous one - neither being able to say to the other what they are thinking about.

'What have you got there?' Desmond is referring to a small carrier bag that Donna is taking with her as she makes to get out of the car.

'These? Referring to a few Co-op plastic bags that she is holding, 'Some things that we might need. I brought these bags from the shop, and I thought that these might be useful too.'

She shows him some of the cellophane gloves that are used in filling stations. She has a clutch of them.

'What are you going to do - fill Joyce up with diesel?'

'Idiot! We have to be prepared. This is serious.'

Desmond does not get it. 'What do you mean?'

'Joyce must not to go to the police tomorrow, agreed?'

'Yes, agreed.'

'So,' Donna continues, 'what if she doesn't agree? What if she insists on going to the police?'

'God! I don't know!'

Donna tries to set this action in a context that even Desmond will understand. 'Apparently, you are a thief.'

'Steady on there!'

'Shut up and listen! You are a thief; we both know it, so let's move on. If Joyce reports you to the police, you will probably go to prison. Then I will be forever be known as the wife of convicted prisoner who stole from a charity shop - and I am not having that.'

'But, what...?'

'Shut up! I could leave you to it. After all, you will have planned for this, won't you? Just how much money do we have for our great escape?'

'Not as much as I would have wished.'

'Exactly! I can't rely on you to fix this; I have to do it myself. There aren't many choices. First choice, and as I have said, still my favourite: I leave you to rot. I am so tempted to do just that, but I know that you're so pathetic that you will even end up making a mess of being a criminal. So, we must try to stop this from happening.'

Donna has that glint in her eye, the glint that says that she is serious.

So is Desmond: 'I have a plan. Not a good one, admittedly.' He wants to contribute, to regain the initiative, but Donna is not having any.

'Too late for plans. We want action - and now. We need more time than Joyce is prepared to give us if we are going to avoid you being arrested. We will go and chat to Joyce; see if she will be reasonable or not. If she insists on following her course of action, we must find the evidence that she has got - those price tags in her handbag.

If we can destroy them, you should be able to talk yourself out of any protests that she makes. Then, if you can be at your most dapper, Joyce the Mouse will stand no chance of being believed!' She smiles at the thought. 'But we need that evidence - and we need to be able to deny that we have been to see Joyce. Hence the gloves - fingerprints!'

'Fingerprints?'

'Of course, fingerprints! We may need to be very careful. We can't leave any evidence that we have been there. So, decline a cup of tea - not that it is going to be offered.'

'What are we going to do? She's going to notice the cellophane gloves, apart from anything else.'

'Idiot! We'll only put them on if we have to touch anything.'

'What do you mean?'

'I am not having that woman ruining my life. It is too late for me - and certainly for you - to run away and start afresh.'

Desmond is taken aback at this. 'Ruining your life? I thought that it was me who was going to prison.'

'My life is resting on the whim of Joyce the Mouse because of you! You are right at the end of the queue from now on. When this is over, I will be leaving you. Understand that.'

At that moment, after explaining what she intends to do when all this is over, Donna comes to a halt mid flow. She has decided: there will be no further conversation.

She takes a long look at her husband who is currently fiddling with a couple of the cellophane gloves. Here is a man who has no idea what is happening, no idea of how he has destroyed any chance that she might have of future happiness. And this same man is waiting - exactly like Option One and Option Two are waiting - for her to decide what must be done.

She was proposing to go herself to clear this mess up, but now she is thinking why the hell should I bother? Nothing will change; this catastrophe is inevitable. No! Enough is enough!

She turns to her husband, 'You know what? Bugger this! Listen carefully. The leaving thing? My options? I'm leaving you - now! I'll not put myself at risk again because of your stupidity. Here! Put your gloves on and go and see Joyce. I'm out of it!'

And she scatters a handful of cellophane gloves over Desmond - like confetti, gives him a little squeeze on the knee and gets out of the car.

She crosses the road to Alfred Hitchcock's, and without glancing back, she walks straight on.

Desmond sits in his car, not sure if he should chase after his wife, not sure that if he did chase her, she would come back with him. If he were to go after her, that might cause a scene - proof that they are in the area. Not a good idea if he still intends to deal with Joyce.

And does he? What does he intend to do? He has no idea any more. There's no point without Donna. She's always been there. Everything he has done, he has done for her, hasn't he?

There must be a better way. He looks towards Alfred Hitchcock's, but Donna has disappeared. He was more than half expecting her to come back to him, after all, she had made her point by flouncing off, but he now knows that there is more to this – much more; lots of new stuff, wrinkles that are now beyond his control.

Maybe she is serious, maybe she has left him.   Confronting her now in a bar full of people is not going to do either of them any good, so he takes a decision. He starts the car, pulls out into the road and drives up the main street towards their home. He drives slowly, glancing in the mirror in the hope that Donna will come chasing after him, but no, that does not happen.

Once home, he decides that he will do what any other condemned man would do. Accepting the inevitable, he finds more than usual comfort in three fingers of his favourite whisky and falls into a doze.

Tomorrow is another day. He will deal with Joyce then. The whisky has told him that it all will be fine, and it will, won't it?

***

That same evening, a few minutes after eleven, two people walk into the little side street of terraced houses where Joyce lives. They have taken great care not to be seen by anyone, and they linger in the shadows for a while, at one point watching another lady, looking very like Joyce, as she returns home from walking her dog. This lady lets herself in to her own home, another Joyce-like terraced house some three or four doors further down the street from their own 'person of interest'.

They have already prepared by calling Joyce's number, explaining the emergency. Joyce is waiting for them and she opens her front door before they even knock.

About twenty minutes later, the same two people leave the house, closing the door quietly and again, making sure that they are not seen. They both remove their cellophane gloves at the same time as they walk around to the marketplace and to a parked car.

Once in the car, they look at the dozens of labels that were once attached to garments on sale in ForGiving. Joyce will not be troubling Desmond and Donna again. Her little old lady's handbag has been emptied of its explosive contents and has been carefully replaced on a shelf next to another similar bag. Neither bag now poses a threat.

Donna looks at her accomplice. Option Two has proved to be a worthy choice.

'You did well,' says Donna, taking his hands in hers. 'Now you deserve your reward.' She leans towards him and meets his lips with hers.

This is Darren, aka Option Two. A confused Darren. Donna has sparked something in him, there is no doubt about that, but the immediate circumstances have somewhat dampened his passion.

He was delighted to receive the phone call earlier in the evening, and dutifully drove off to meet Donna outside Alfred Hitchcock's where she was waiting for him. Her promise, now to be realised, was her decision that it was to be him. She had made her choice. Desmond was out; from now on it was to be Darren and Donna. They would be together from now on - if he was still interested.

Given that since Donna first intimated to him the possibility some days ago, that she might - just might - be up for it, Darren has been in a permanent state of arousal. This, he feels, is a pretty good state for a man of fifty-odd, and he was hopeful that tonight Donna's promise will come true, not in the car park of the market place, but back in his bungalow - in his specially decorated bedroom with the ambient lighting and the James Last soundtrack in the background. Oh yes, and those 'marital aids' as they used to call them, that he has never had the opportunity to try out - yet.

Now Donna's lips, and the insistent demands of her tongue might well have sent him over the edge there and then - were it not for the immediate circumstances - and the fact that he has recently murdered somebody.

'What the hell have we done?' Darren's response to the kiss is not as Donna expected, and his first words kill the intended mood immediately.

Donna tries to recoup the situation, 'We had to do it, darling. She was an evil woman and - and if we hadn't, she was going to hurt someone very badly.'

'Who?'

'It doesn't matter.'

'It bloody does matter! And what are these things for?' He picks up a few of the price tags and tries to make some sense of what was going on.

'They are for something else. I needed to get them - for another purpose.'

'Two birds with one stone - with one plastic bag, I mean. What have we done? What have I done?'

'I told you that I needed your help. I had to have your help. But now it's over, and you and I can go back to yours - and I will make it up to you. I will make it up to you - tonight.'

And her lips meet his once again. Truth be told, Darren's not that interested now, although his heart is pumping, and his nerves are jangling like never before. It feels like a sexual thing. It's been a while, but when he was a younger man, he can remember feeling exactly like this. The anticipation, the hope - the slight feeling of concern in case it didn't all work out as planned.

The feelings that he has now are as he remembers them - but with one slight difference. They are nothing to do with sex. His mind is fixated not on the prospect of Donna, but on the bird-like little lady whose arms he pinned to her side while Donna put that bag - it was a Co-op bag, for God's sake - over her wispy grey hair, covering her terrified face and her uncomprehending, staring eyes.

He is the one who held her still while Donna fastened the bag around her throat and tightened it with the knot. To cap it all, it was he who held her in her death throes while Donna was searching through her handbags to get those ridiculous little bits of paper. And she was bloody strong - she was difficult to hang on to - kneeing him in the balls and almost knocking the wind out of him. But he held on, held on until the struggles started to subside. Donna came to check that she was dead, holding a clutch of labels in her hand, and saying that they had better get going.

As they are leaving the house, Darren watches the woman who has turned him into a murderer checking that everything is neat and tidy. What he does not see is the paper tissue that she has slipped under the lifeless body on the floor. What he does see is that she is smiling at him in a curious way. Someone once said that the Mona Lisa's smile was the smile of a woman who had just eaten her husband. It is that kind of smile.

How the hell did he get into this mess? 'What the f*** have I done?' The reality is beginning to sink in.

'Shhh! Don't worry. You are with me now. I'll look after you. I always keep my promises. Come on, start the car - take me home.' And he does.

Darren's bungalow is set back from the road in an area outside of Ambleton and known as Under Loughrigg. His private drive of two hundred metres or so leads to a comfortable, modern two-bedroomed home. He has no neighbours to overlook the house, and this suits him fine. Darren has never wanted neighbours and has yet to make any friends in the immediate vicinity.

Yes, he has joined the masons, and enjoys the odd game of bowls, but he has always chosen his level of participation carefully, thinking that if he were to hit it off with a new partner - or more likely - if he were to get the occasional full-body massage with a happy ending - or maybe a lady of the night to visit him, the no neighbour policy would pay off handsomely.

And so it has. He and Donna arrive at his house not having seen a soul on the short drive. No cars either. He pulls up outside the side door, and he and Donna go into the kitchen. The blinds are already closed, the ambient lighting perfectly moderated - and James Last is playing on a loop in the background.

'This is beautiful,' says Donna, 'truly beautiful, Darren. You have such good taste and I do like that in a man.'

'Taste? You've noticed my good taste? We are both killers! We are going to spend the rest of our lives in prison. You know that don't you?'

'Not if you keep quiet, we aren't. There is nothing to tie us to Joyce, and I am pretty sure that we left no trace either. The gloves worked a treat!'

Donna looks around the room. 'Do we have something to drink, darling?'

They do, they certainly do. Although it is not exactly his first choice, Darren being a real ale man, he has put a bottle of Prosecco in the fridge - in anticipation. He gets a couple of glasses down from the cupboard, pops the wine open and pours it into the glasses.

'Good choice, darling,' says Donna. 'Prosecco always does it for me. Take me to your room now. I am in your debt - and I mean to repay you.'

Darren feels a stirring that this time is definitely sexual in origin, and he opens the door to the bedroom. Donna looks around, sees the en-suite and says, 'Give me a couple of minutes. Get into bed and wait for me.'

Darren says, 'I need to go to ...' But she has gone, so he moves to the second bathroom, relieves himself, has a cursory wash and takes a swig from his mouthwash as he doesn't want his halitosis to spoil things. Not now, not after all this - fuss. No, whatever happens after this, he deserves his - reward.

He gets into bed - wearing only his underpants, as Donna comes out of the bathroom. She is in black, a lacy bra and pants setting off her toned and tanned body. A red silk scarf rippling as she moves towards him. Darren has to admit to himself that she still looks pretty fit, and he recalls a chat show programme on the radio where the topic was, 'Madonna - would you?' He's not sure that he would - Madonna, that is, but looking at his Donna standing there - the ambient lighting working a treat - his body tells him that in this situation, yes, he will!

Donna gets into bed with him, snuggling up and reaching for him. 'I want you - I have wanted you for such a long time.'

'I never dreamed - not true - I did dream, did nothing but dream for months, but I never thought that you'd ...'

Donna squeezes him gently, 'I did. I really did, but I wanted to be sure of you. Sorry you had to wait. I had to wait too. All those nights spent knowing that I should have been spending them with you. What a waste! But we can make up for it now.'

And their lovemaking begins. As they start, each is slow and considerate; after all, neither is in the first flush of youth, and the memories of an hour ago could easily dampen anybody's passion. Darren checks, like men do, and he is pleased that so far, the Cialis is holding up to the job required of it.

After a few minutes of ever more powerful caressing, Donna murmurs, 'Do you have any toys, Darren?'

'What kind of toys are you thinking about?'

'Oh, I don't know. That bedhead is going to waste - it's so strong, and I do have a fantasy...'

Darren is in heaven: 'What did you have in mind?'

She whispers to him, 'I want you to tie me up and then spank me. That's my fantasy.'

'You like that?'

'I love that - it makes me come like a train.'

Holding that thought alone means that Darren has no further need to check his prowess, probably no further need for Cialis either. And he does have a couple of pairs of pink fluffy handcuffs in the bedside cabinet. They are perfect for an occasion such as this, bought on Amazon, but never used. (Incidentally, he has also carried a condom in his wallet - just in case - for over twenty years! Never had the opportunity!)

He's not going to waste this one, though. He asks Donna what she would like him to do.

'I want you to cuff me to the bedhead, put a mask on me, spank me red raw and then make me come!'

The mask is improvised from Donna's silk scarf, tied tightly, but perfectly serviceable, and they begin.

Darren does turn out to be a little over-enthusiastic in the spanking department, and Donna has to ask him to tone things down a little. She asks him more than once to stop it; after the latest bout of enthusiasm, she has to shout, 'Stop! Stop it, For F**** sake - you're hurting me!'

But his enthusiasm achieves Donna's objective - and for the first time in a long time, her train thunders through the station!

Donna lies still and sated. She feels so complete, so utterly satisfied that she never wants to move from that spot. But Darren is still eager; his train has not yet departed.

'Undo me darling,' she says. 'God, that was wonderful - you were wonderful. Now it's your turn!'

'My turn?'

'Yes, your turn. That was everything that I could have dreamed of - everything. I want to do the same for you - and then you are going to do me again, and maybe again after that!'

She rubs her wrists. 'You did like that, didn't you?'

'I've never done anything ...'

'I know,' She slips her tongue gently into his mouth. 'And you will be amazed when I do the same for you, I promise. You deserve your reward.'

Darren is not sure if Mr Cialis will be able to stand up for the long haul, but he is certainly building up a head of steam.

'What do I do?'

'You lie back and enjoy - that's not going to be too difficult, is it? Do you want me to spank you?'

'Mmm I'm not sure. No, I think no...'

'That's ok my darling, I understand. So just lie there and relax. Let me do all the work. I want to make this the best sex that you have ever had.'

'It already is!'

'I know, Precious, I know. But you must wait a just little longer. We're thinking of a higher division now, and you've been promoted!'

She lies him down, puts a pillow behind his head and asks, 'Do you have any handkerchiefs?'

'Yes, why?'

'You see these marks on my wrists? I don't want you to be hurting afterwards. I'll put a handkerchief there to stop the handcuffs rubbing.'

'You are going to use them on me?'

'Of course, I am!' She smiles as she kisses him, 'That's where the joy comes from. If I control everything, your orgasm will be stronger than anything you have ever experienced before.' She giggles, and then says, 'We'll probably have to wipe down the ceiling.'

Darren smiles back at her sheepishly. 'Unlikely' is what he is thinking, but he doesn't say so. Maybe once upon a time? Nevertheless, he's as excited as he has ever been, and is happy to make do with that.

He lies back while Donna puts a handkerchief and then a handcuff around each wrist, fastening them both to the sturdy metal bedhead that has so recently afforded her so much pleasure.

Once again, she uses her silk scarf as a makeshift mask, this time for him, and she begins to attend to Darren's needs. Her lips and her tongue slowly making their way down his body. She stops.

'What's wrong?' Darren whimpers. He can't contain himself for much longer.

'I'm want to sit on your face, darling. And after that, I need you inside me. But I want to control your every movement. Do you have a belt?'

'A belt? Yes, in the top drawer, over there.'

'Wait!' She gets up from the bed and moves to the chest of drawers that Darren has indicated. There, she sees a selection of rather natty belts, at least five or six of them, all curled up like snakes and very tidily arranged. She selects two.

'What are you doing?'

'I want to make this perfect, my love. I want you to be completely helpless when I sit on you, and then when we make love, you can abandon yourself to the moment, knowing that there is nothing you can do except enjoy it.'

She takes Darren's ankle, kisses it and gently loops a belt around it. She then ties the belt to the metal bar at the foot of the bed. She does the same thing to the other foot, so Darren is now masked and tied to the four corners of the bed - a starfish with a giant erection!

'Now my lovely man. See how you like this!' She moves towards him, straddling his chest and inching herself towards his waiting mouth. As his tongue reaches out for her, he can no longer hold himself in, and his shuddering climax begins.

When Donna puts the plastic bag over his head, it is a couple of seconds or so before he realises what is going on. The bitch! She's doing the same thing to me! And she is. His shoulders are pinned down by Donna's ample hips - all the two of them now need is a wrestling referee to count 'One - Two - Three' for the bout to be won and Donna declared the winner.

There is no referee, but there is a winner. Donna is quite used to the asphyxiation process now, and she waits for all the fuss to die down before she moves away from the now quite still body of Darren.

She works quickly. Wearing another pair of cellophane gloves, she finds a roll of plastic bin liners and she places each object that she has used: including the handcuffs, handkerchiefs and the two belts into two of them. The handcuffs, she remembers, were exactly the same kind as she and Desmond used to play with. Happy days!

All the clothing that Darren had on when they arrived at his house also goes into one of the bin bags.

She spends some careful minutes stripping the bed – working around the body, rolling it backwards and forwards. The duvet is folded tight, tied even more tightly with two more of Darren's belts and is too placed into a bin bag, along with the fitted bottom sheet and four pillowcases.

Darren now receives the most meticulous bed bath that any man has ever received in the history of the world. Every patch of skin, every orifice and each crack and fold is cleaned, first with soap and water and then again with fresh clean water. She pats her man down with a towel and is pleased with herself that she has not allowed any water to seep into the mattress. The towel also goes into the bin liner.

She unties the plastic bag and removes it from around her lover's head. In doing so, Donna experiences a pang of regret, but only a pang. The sex was good, but there will be other men - and much more sex - now that she has liberated herself. The silk scarf, which has performed such a useful function as a mask, is also retrieved.

She thoroughly cleans his head, using cotton buds to get into his ears, his nose and around his eyes. She opens his mouth and carefully wipes as much of the mouth, teeth and tongue as she can, certain that all trace of her is removed.

She finishes the job with Darren's own roll-on anti-perspirant, *Tabac,* which she finds in the bathroom cabinet. She applies it liberally to his armpits, his crotch and to his hair. He does smell good, even if she says so herself. She has always liked *Tabac*. Maybe that was the clincher?

Next, she goes to the linen cupboard in the hallway, finds an array of sheets, pillowcases, duvets - all waiting for her to choose. She takes the four pillows from the bed and finds room for two of them in each of her bin bags. She then takes four new pillows - still in their plastic wrappings - from the linen cupboard and puts a new pillowcase on each of them; the plastic wrappings themselves carefully placed in one of the bin bags.

Moving Darren's body as needed, she fashions a well-made bed, on which he is now lying.

The pyjamas are something of a challenge, but she is strong, and Darren is still quite flexible. She places him in a sleeping position and looks at him. There is the slightest of marks around each of his ankles, but nothing at all on his wrists.

She gets a pair of socks from the drawer and puts them on him. Men often sleep with their socks on, don't they? Especially if there is no woman around to keep an eye on them. The top of the sock is adjusted to match the marks that are concerning her. Now they look much more natural: the marks could have been made by the socks being that little bit too tight.

Darren himself looks comfortable, and as far as she can see, there is no sign of any violent activity. She knows nothing about what happens at a post-mortem, other than what she has seen on the telly. She supposes that a wizard pathologist would be able to work out what has happened, but with no obvious signs, would they bother? And when is he going to be found? He's no relatives that she knows of, and he was proud to tell Donna that he didn't have any neighbours. He's a fifty-odd year-old man who has died in his sleep, isn't he?

Is it worth her taking the risk? Will they conduct a post-mortem anyway, what with the cuts to their budgets and all? She thinks it unlikely, and there are not too many alternatives available: it had to be done this way.

Nevertheless, there might be a post-mortem if, for example, Darren is found quite soon. So, she decides to take one more risk. From her pocket, she takes a small clear envelope and from that she removes a single small hair. She places the hair under Darren's tongue and closes his mouth, settling him into his final sleeping position with a peck on the cheek - which, not for posterity, but for her own safety, she immediately wipes off.

Her final task is to clean all the surfaces that she has touched. She knows exactly where those surfaces are so this only takes a moment or two. She switches the lights off in the bedroom, leaving only the night light in the hallway. James Last playing away in the background has also been disposed of. She reflects that James Last might have been an impediment to their future relationship.

She lets herself out of the house, carrying the two bin bags and the price tags that have been such a pain in the arse for her. She carries nothing else and is quite pleased about that as the two bags, while not particularly heavy are more cumbersome than she would have wished. There is no security lighting to trouble her, and she begins the long walk home.

One single car slowly passing her by is the only sign of movement that she sees; its headlights in the distance giving her plenty of time to avoid being seen.

She is very pleased that Darren had bought heavy-duty bin bags: those thin things that she used at home would certainly not have been fit for purpose.

***

'Wake up, you lazy bugger! Let me in!' It is the knocking, not the shouting that wakes Desmond from his whisky sleep. He looks out of the bedroom window and sees Donna's smiling face.

'Well, are you going to let me in?'

'What? I thought you'd left me. Where've you been?'

He goes quickly downstairs, opens the door and sees Donna standing there; two full bin bags next to her.

From her pocket, she hands him a pile of price tags. 'Here you are. Job done!'

'Where did you get these from?'

'Where do you think?'

'Joyce?'

'Yup.'

'She just gave them to you, did she?'

'What do you think?'

'Oh.'

'Take me to bed.'

'What?'

'Take me to bed. I need to have sex with you - now!'

'Donna, I'm not sure that ...'

'Oh yes you can. And you will!'

***

Next day, Desmond and Donna are in bed having their morning cup of tea.

Can I ask something? You know when you went in to Alfred's last night?'

'Yes.'

'Did anybody see you?'

'Of course not - I didn't go in. I walked around to Millans Park - and I met a friend.'

'Did anybody see you with - your friend?'

'No, we sat in the car for a while and then we went for a drive. That's the real version. Did anyone see you last night?'

'I don't think so, no.'

'Good. So, this is the new real version. We went home together, you had a few whiskies, we had some good sex - if anyone asks - and you will go into work this morning. Ok?'

'If you say so.'

90

'I do say so. No variation, do you understand? Right! I'm off shopping. Who's on today?

'Joyce.'

'Oh,' says Donna, not quite sure how to proceed with the conversation. Then she decides, 'Good! Maybe she'll turn up. If she doesn't, I'll come in and help until lunchtime.'

She gives her husband a kiss on the cheek, then says, 'One other thing - don't worry! I'm pretty sure that Joyce won't trouble us anymore. If we are going to leave Ambleton, and by the way, I don't intend to, we can take our time. No decisions of any kind will be made today.'

Desmond makes to ask, and Donna places a finger over his lips. 'Don't ask. You don't need to know. It's gone - the evidence. There is no evidence anymore. Oh, and Joyce probably won't be coming in.'

***

A little later, having arrived at ForGiving, Desmond is thinking about how he might open the shop. No volunteers have arrived. Mickey comes in the door.

'Hi Desmond, I've come to see Joyce. Is she in yet?

Desmond, having already been coached by his wife, has modelled his response to this question - although he didn't expect it to be Mickey who is doing the asking.

'I don't know if she is coming in, Mickey. She was supposed to be here ages ago. She hasn't phoned, either. Maybe she is ill. What did you want to see her about?'

'Oh. It doesn't matter. It can wait.'

'You are not normally here on a Friday.'

'No. I had things to do.'

'And have you done them?'

'Not really. I'll try again later.'

'You couldn't help me out and work the morning shift, could you? Or at least until Joyce comes in? I'll get someone to take over from you for the afternoon, I promise. Donna has offered to come in later.'

'I suppose I could; I am here anyway.'

'Great! I've stacks of paperwork to do. I'll be in the back if you need me. You are ok to work until one o'clock?'

'I'll need to leave just before one so that I can catch my bus.'

'Of course, yes. You are a life saver! Thanks.' And Mickey begins to serve the first customers who have come into the shop.

As agreed, he works the morning shift, and leaves to catch his bus home a little before one.

Towards the end of the afternoon, Desmond receives a telephone call from the police, and he turns to Donna who has been happily working with him since she returned to the shop after lunch.

'That was the police.'

'The police? Why?'

'Kendal police calling on behalf of Mickey - they put him on the line because he wanted to speak to me. It was his one telephone call, he said. The one that he was allowed to make. Joyce has been murdered - and he's been arrested.'

'She's been murdered? How? When?'

'I've no idea. He didn't say, but I suppose the police will be around here soon. Then we'll find out. He wanted me to help him. I said that I didn't want anything to do with a murderer.'

'I heard what you said. Sometimes I think that you are not just dense, you are deliberately stupid.'

'What do you mean?'

'You don't think, do you? A murder investigation involving one of your staff? If Mickey has done something awful like that, you could at least pretend to be supportive. He does look up to you, you know.

'It will do you no harm if you can be seen as the wise head of the team, showing suitable concern for one of your people. We need all the friends that we can get, and he's always been on your side. Get a grip, Desmond. Get a grip!'

'I have never spoken to a murderer before; I don't know the protocol.'

'I despair! Honestly you never cease to amaze me!'

***

Desmond's various disaster scenarios have yet to unravel, and he is beginning to think that maybe they won't. It's been a few weeks now, and after Mickey was released from custody without charge, no further arrests have been made.

With no Joyce on her mission to destroy him, Desmond has been able to get back to slicing the ForGiving takings even more in his favour, and the financial meltdown that he once thought to be inevitable has not yet happened.

Because of internal logistical reasons, the head office at ForGiving has had to put off its audit of the Ambleton shop for a few weeks. There is real breathing space here, and D&D are able to plan the next stage of their lives with a little less urgency.

About four weeks after Joyce's death, the local paper, the Westmorland Gazette, runs a short article. The decomposing body of a man believed to be in his fifties was found at a house on Under Loughrigg. The police named him, and the newspaper mentioned that he had recently retired to Ambleton from Blackpool, where he had previously run a business.

He had no next of kin, and he had apparently not made any close friends in the area. No-one had noticed that he wasn't around, and as he received very little post, the box at the end of drive gave no indication.

It was an engineer from a utilities company who eventually phoned the police. Coming to the house for the third time to fit a smart meter, and noticing the car parked outside, he had gone up to the front door and called through the letter box by the door. The smell emanating from the house - oozing through the double glazing and the insulated walls - had given him all the signals that he needed. Back at ForGiving, life - apart from the deaths obviously goes on D&D have an uneasy truce: neither wants to go back to their former state, but they have tacitly agreed to stay together for now.

Donna, because of the possibilities offered by her brief but educative flirtations, has decided to look for a better future than her husband can offer. Desmond, oblivious to Donna's change of focus, still wants to 'move on' and try something new, anything new. Their former world, their habitual and expected behaviours, will never be the same again.

Detective Inspector Max Wordsworth

'So, what about your cereal? Do you just leave it?' The young man looks up from his breakfast tray to ask the question.

'What do you mean?'

The young man continues, 'Why don't you start with your cereal?'

Max Wordsworth finishes his mouthful of bacon and egg, looks around the room and then addresses his colleague. 'Buffet breakfast – always eat the hot stuff first.'

'Bit strange, don't you think?'

'Otherwise there's no point in having a hot breakfast! It's a cold breakfast, then, isn't it? If I must pile everything on a tray, to save walking up and down to the buffet, I always eat the hot stuff first. I'll enjoy the delicious cereal, and the healthy fruit option too, but in a few moments. Is that ok with you?'

'With me? Yes, of course. Sorry! I was a little surprised.'

'We'll chat again about my breakfast eating preferences any time you wish, just let me know.'

'Sorry sir!'

DI Max Wordsworth smiles, breaks the ice that is starting to encase his detective constable, 'No more 'sorry'. Don't apologise. You are too easy to wind up, Martin. Let's get on with our breakfast and then get out of here.'

They arrived last night, up from Preston, and are going to begin the investigation later this morning. Their hotel has turned out to be surprisingly comfortable, even though it is on the main drag through Ambleton. Views of the lake from each of their rooms, coffee machine and free WIFI. All in all, a pretty good choice, and so unlike the kind of accommodation that is normally provided when police officers are deployed away from home.

Wordsworth has brought his young assistant, the twenty-five-year-old, recently promoted Detective Constable Martin Tomlinson because he wants to get this job finished as soon as possible, and then get back down to Lancashire to do some proper policing. He doesn't like trying to fix the mistakes of colleagues. Try as he might to be professional about the whole process, there is always something unsavoury about having to take a colleague - or colleagues - to task for their incompetence.

'What looks to be a murder investigation, badly botched with some bloke arrested immediately, and then let go. There's also the possibility of a suspicious death too.'

Tomlinson looks across the table towards his boss, 'Suspicious death? Any connection?'

'Here's the thing. There is a connection - of a sort. And that's why we are here in Ambleton. We've been given the old police station - we can walk around to it from here - and we have one week or so before people start shouting 'budget' at me. But before then, I want to finish my breakfast, if that's all right with you.'

'Of course, sir. But I did want to thank you for bringing me here with you.'

'There is a reason for that too.'

'Oh?' Tomlinson is intrigued.

'My name.'

'Your name? Oh, Wordsworth?'

'It's not a really big deal, but it does annoy me. It's one of the reasons I hate coming here. I don't like poetry and I know next to nothing about the other bloke with my name who used to live up here. Everybody assumes. Ok? So, if they ask, and they will, you will provide a calming influence - and you'll be doing most of the spade work too. So, let's move on and get this case sorted asap.'

'Yes sir. Of course. More coffee?'

'Why not? We are not expected until ten.'

The rest of breakfast is conducted in relative silence; each police officer reflecting on why he has been called up from Preston, and what the possible ramifications of this investigation might be.

While Max stays in the dining room for yet another coffee and a glance at the newspaper, Martin pops upstairs to call his girlfriend. He shares with her as much information as he can, which in truth is very little, and tries to reassure her that it is work and only work that requires him to stay away from her for a few nights, and no, he is not going off her.

The old police station on the Rydal Road is much better equipped than either Max or Martin has expected. Until recently, it has been staffed by a civilian for three or four days a week and visited regularly by passing uniform patrols as they were driving by. It is clean, quiet, and has retained its small computer system - although a call has recently come for that to be moved down to Kendal, as the building is going to be put up for sale.

The police house next door was sold off years ago and is now a holiday home for a couple from Droitwich. The remaining part of the building, complete with its own one-person cell, will easily convert into another holiday let in the middle of the town, a town which is increasingly full of similar holiday lets. It has long been impossible for local people to buy property here.

'A kettle and a fridge - with milk in it! And somebody has left us coffee and tea.'

'Who do we thank for that? Max looked around, but there is nobody in the office.

'That would be me,' a female voice chimes in. 'I thought you wouldn't mind.'

'Mind?' said Max, turning round to see the young woman who has introduced herself by interrupting, standing in the doorway. 'That was kind, thank you.'

'You will probably appreciate these, then.' And she places a paper bag on the desk. 'Freshly baked from the 'Apple Pie'.' She points, 'over there, past the

Bridge House. You'll enjoy working here - at least you can eat well. I'm Helen, Helen Lang, and I am your new admin assistant.'

'I'm Max, DI Wordsworth, and this is Martin, DC Tomlinson.'

'Wordsworth? Are you any relation to William?'

'See what I mean?' says Max, turning towards his DC.

'Yes sir.' His smile of understanding seems to confuse Helen for a moment, but then Martin gives her his full attention. 'I'm pleased to meet you, Helen,' says Martin as he shakes the hand of the attractive twenty-something blonde who has just made his - and Max's day. 'Thanks for these, too. It was - as he said - a lovely gesture.' And he smiles as he opens the paper bag.

'My treat, but only for today. You'll have to pay for them from tomorrow, but I'll be happy to go and get them for you - if you wish.'

'We'd better get started. Sort yourself a desk, Martin.' Max sits down at what will become his workstation. 'I'll work here. Are you ok over there, Helen?'

'That's fine sir - next to the kettle, I see.'

'Ha! Pure coincidence. Young DC Tomlinson will make as many cups of tea and coffee as you while we are here.'

'Where are you based?' Martin asks.

'Kendal police station. I've worked there for three years.'

Max picks up on this, 'I knew that you had worked for the police for three years; I didn't realise that you were based in Kendal.'

'Oh, were you not informed?'

'No.' Suddenly the mood has changed, and all three people sense it. Max continues, his tone of voice no longer quite so light and friendly. 'This has to be done now. There is no other way. Can I formalise matters for a moment?'

'What do you mean, sir?'

Max looks towards his young assistant, 'Sit down please, Helen. Introductions over, gifts of cakes thankfully accepted. You've received your brief, I assume?'

'Yes.'

'And does the brief clarify your roles and responsibilities?'

'Yes sir, I think so.'

'So, I need to make some things clear before we begin. I don't yet know the direction in which we will be going, but the people that we may end up investigating, possibly for incompetence, unprofessional conduct and maybe more, are most likely to be people who work out of Kendal. Some of them may be your colleagues.'

'I am aware of that sir. I am familiar with the details of the case.'

'You see my point, then?'

Helen frowns, 'I think I do. You are suggesting that because I work out of Kendal, I might not act professionally.'

'As long as we understand each other.'

'I think we do. Is that what you are thinking?'

'Not yet, no. As I said, I want to make it clear, so that if you feel that you may have a conflict of interest, you can walk away now. This is a delicate case to begin with. I am surprised that admin help has come from Kendal and not from elsewhere. It could cause problems. It's important that we understand each other from the outset.'

'And we do,' replies Helen. 'This assignment is something that I volunteered for. I typed the original reports, and I am familiar with the case. I want to see it resolved too. I am on your side, sir. But, if you feel otherwise, I am quite happy to go back to Kendal and we could try to arrange for someone else to come up to work with you, maybe from a different office.'

Max looks carefully at Helen, seems to be weighing up his options, and then says, 'Not necessary. I don't think that either of us would like to lose you.' Martin nods in enthusiastic agreement, although he is motivated by different considerations: this woman is beautiful!

Max motors on, 'This is a worrying case, and I wanted to make it clear how important our integrity will be to its success. So, with that out of the way, let's get started - oh, and thank you again for the cakes.'

'Martin adds, 'Yes, thanks Helen, you've made us feel welcome.'

Helen is wary, but she makes her way to what is now to be her desk, and while she's slightly miffed at the DI's attitude, she probably sees his point.

'So, let's see where we are, shall we?' Max picks up the first of a number of files that are on his desk, opens it and says, 'Almost four weeks ago now, Miss Joyce Todd, sixty-seven years of age. Found dead at her home by her cleaning lady early on a Friday morning. Joyce normally worked at a charity shop on Fridays. The shop is called 'ForGiving'.

'Police on the scene within twenty minutes of the body being found; CID 35 minutes later. The crime scene was closed off and Forensics arrived at 1030.'

'So far, so good,' Martin's remark stops Max's train of thought.

'But! There's always a 'but' in these circumstances, and that's why we are here.' After giving Martin a long look, he continues: 'And this, apparently, is where the wheels come off. The investigating officer looks at the Co-op bag that has been used to asphyxiate the victim and notices some fingerprints on it.

'He's just downloaded an exciting new app on his phone - and so he thinks, why not, I'll use it! Totally inappropriately, as it turns out.'

'How do you mean, sir?'

'It's still a prototype - fingerprint recognition, a brilliant piece of kit, apparently. On his smartphone; linked to the PNC. We'll all be using it soon, I reckon. But not yet. Early adopters always get it wrong. The officer photographed the prints on the bag with his new app, and Bingo! It worked! They had a man in custody that same day, and the investigation's great success was trumpeted everywhere that weekend.

'Sadly, the man they arrested wasn't the perpetrator, and he was released after an embarrassing weekend. And now, four weeks later, we are asked, DC

Tomlinson and me, to come up from Preston and see if we can move things forward.'

Helen asks, 'Why has it taken so long?'

Max says, 'Politics is involved, lawyers are involved and this time, bearing in mind the debacle of the first arrest, local CID had hoped to be able to clear it up quietly. That didn't happen, and the Independent Police Complaints Commission became got wind of it. The IPCC then requested our presence - not the guy who was wrongly arrested - more politics, I guess.'

'Do we have any suspects?' Tomlinson asks his boss.

'Helen, do we have any suspects?'

'No sir, we don't. The man, Michael 'Mickey' Hembrow, was released as his alibi was sound. But we do have some leads - or at least, some possible lines of enquiry.'

'And they are?'

Helen looks at her file, 'Firstly, there's definitely a connection with this shop, ForGiving. Joyce Todd worked there, and Mickey, Michael Hembrow, the original suspect, works there too. He is adamant that the Co-op bag - the bag with his prints on it - could also have come from there; as he often uses bags like that to take his stuff to and from the shop.'

'Does he still work there?'

'Yes, sir. After he was released, he insisted on returning. The manager wasn't very pleased, but the DI originally in charge of the case had a word.'

'Ok, thanks. What do we know about the crime itself?'

Helen glances at the notes in front of her and begins to read them from the beginning. As she does, Max stops her with a gesture and says, 'The gist, please. That will be enough.'

'Yes sir. The victim was killed by having a plastic Co-op bag placed over her head, a bag which was then tied tightly and knotted. There were no scratch marks, no bruises or anything at all to suggest that she had put up a fight. The assumption seems to be that she was held down, or that her arms were pinioned by someone. She was a tiny woman, and quite frail. A strong person could have held her still until she died.'

'This was the work of one person?' DC Tomlinson is trying to create a picture of the incident.

'The report suggests that it was more likely that at least two people were involved.'

'Why?'

'Logic - and it's only supposition; there's no proof that there were two people - or more - involved. However, Joyce was fully dressed, so it is unlikely that she was asleep when she was attacked.'

Helen explains the conclusions of the report in front of her, 'A sneak thief could have surprised her in bed, or while she was asleep, and then sat on her until she died. That's one possibility. But the report here says that because she was fully dressed, and because she was found downstairs with no marks or scratches on her, it is more likely that one person held her tightly with her arms by her sides, while the other put the bag over her head and tied it. She would then have been held until she could struggle no more.'

Max comments, 'They said that they thought that two people were involved but seem to have been happy when they arrested one. And because they were so sure that they had got their man, the initial investigation seems to have petered out. There was a forensic examination of the crime scene, and some door-to-door interviews, but nothing much has shown up so far.'

Max lifts his head from the file and asks, 'Helen, do you know this 'ForGiving' place?'

'Yes, it's not far from here. It's been there for years. The people who work there are all volunteers, apart from a part-time manager who works two or three days a week. I often pop in when I am in Ambleton. They have some good stuff, if you are not too fussy. And the clothes they sell are always clean.'

Martin adds, 'I buy loads of things from charity shops, always have. And before you say it, sir - not this suit. This is not just a suit, it is a M&S suit, I'll have you know.'

Max smiles and doesn't make the wisecrack that was on the tip of his tongue. Instead he says, 'Mickey and Joyce both worked there, but apparently on different days. Mickey said in his interview that he didn't know her. They had hardly ever met; they worked on different days and were only in the same room together for occasional meetings, and then they never spoke to each other. But there was also something about poison pen notes - what was that?'

'Yes, I remember! Give me a moment - there is something.' Helen flicks through some pages. 'Here! There were some threatening notes found in Mickey's bedsit in Winstermere. He had collected about ten of them over the preceding weeks. He said that they were placed in the shop for him to find when he came into work, and he found at least one of them delivered to his house in Winstermere.'

'Did he mention them to anyone?'

'Apparently, he wanted to tell his manager, but said that he didn't dare. He didn't know whether the manager would have been of any help. He also said that he was sure that it was Joyce who had written them - they were in her handwriting. So, he had intended to confront her, and had come into Ambleton that Friday morning to do it, but although he was at the shop waiting for her, she never turned up. Ironically, he ended up working Joyce's shift for her, and when he got home, he was arrested for her murder.'

Martin says, 'If she had written those notes, it would have given him a motive.'

Helen shakes her head, 'Maybe, but it didn't happen. CCTV on the Ambleton to Winstermere bus places Mickey exactly where and when he said he was. He has no transport of his own, not even a bike. It wasn't him.'

'He could easily have come back to Ambleton on the Thursday evening. No friend with a car?'

'No friend, full stop. Mickey has no friends. He's one of those lonely men. The ForGiving shop seems to be his only connection with the outside world – apart from a person across the road who sometimes keeps an eye on his dog.'

'But he did have a motive.'

'He did!' Max interrupts, 'Yes, he had a motive, or thinks he did. Obviously, if it wasn't him, there's somebody else out there also with a motive. We've got to look elsewhere, and the ForGiving shop seems to be the centre of this particular universe.'

Helen adds - looking at her file - 'There's another death that's also linked to ForGiving. I don't know if there is a connection, but the husband of another of the volunteers, someone who lived near Sizergh - quite a way from here - he was found dead in the gym in the basement of his house around about the same time. It seems like it was a tragic accident, barbells across his throat choked him. They must have slipped. There is no official suggestion of foul play, but the wife is also a volunteer at ForGiving. Probably a coincidence.'

'Nevertheless!' Max makes to comment, but the thought is left in mid-air as Martin says, 'There was something in the paper about that. Wasn't he in trouble with the police?'

Helen answers, 'He was head teacher of a special school near Churchfield. Due in court sometime soon. He and five or six others, all teachers at his special needs school, they've been charged with various sexual offences against children.'

'Does the report suggest any connection?' Max is keen to establish whether this incident may have any bearing on Joyce's murder.

'Other than his wife and Joyce were volunteers at the same shop, no, I don't believe that the report suggests any connection at all.'

'Right!' Max wants to move on. 'If that is the case, we can come back to that later. You have her details in that file?'

'Yes, sir.'

'Good. Now let's think about Joyce Todd. What do we know about her?'

'She retired up here about ten years ago. From Liverpool. Single, no family that we were able to trace.'

The cynic in Max says, 'If she owned her house, and with prices being what they are locally, there'll be somebody coming out of the woodwork soon, you can bet on that!'

Helen shuffles through the papers in her file. 'She worked as a floor walker, store detective, in a big department store for over twenty years - interesting occupation?'

'Martin, can we check if there are any reports of her being harassed? Did anybody cause her concern? How did she get on with her neighbours and did she express any worries to anybody?

'Yes, sir, but hasn't that been done already?'

Helen adds: 'Everybody in the area was questioned, sir. Those questions were all answered. We have the transcripts here - if you wish to see them.'

There is silence. Quite an embarrassing silence. Then Max breaks it, 'You realise that I am looking for a way into this. I don't mind that you are knocking me back...'

Helen is the first to respond, 'I'm not knocking you back, sir. It's because...' Martin follows, 'It's not ...'

'I know, I know! Let me put it another way. You have all the files relating to the investigation, and everything we have looked at so far shows that due process was carried out. That's true, isn't it?

'I have already had sight of most of the documentation that you are referring to, and what you have said - what you have both said, in your own way, is that everything was done properly. Yes? But it wasn't, was it? The wrong man was arrested, the police were made to look like idiots, and there is a murderer walking around now - and we've no idea who the hell it is!

'I am not asking for this information so that you can show me how well you can read. I am asking you to try to see things differently, to look for gaps, hints, suggestions that we might explore; suggestions that have not already been acted upon. It's the Einstein thing.'

'Sir?' Martin has completely lost that plot.

'Einstein and his other theory - the madness one. He is supposed to have said that the definition of madness is 'doing the same thing day after day and expecting it to be different tomorrow'. That's what we are doing. Everything was done correctly; all is in order - but the result is complete bollocks! So, we've got to look at things differently.'

Slightly abashed, Martin says, 'Yes sir. Helen, let me have a look at the files that you have. Here, you take these from me.'

As they are swapping files, Martin says, 'You know, there is one thing.'

'And that is?'

'Those poison pen notes - the notes that Mickey had at home?'

'What about them?'

'Have they been checked out? Were they even written by Joyce?'

'Helen?' Max looks toward his young admin assistant who says, 'No sir, I've not seen anything that suggests that they were checked out. They weren't followed up, no - here, this says that 'a number of hand-written notes, all of an offensive nature, were found at the suspect's house.' That's all - they were not followed up. I suppose that once Mickey had been cleared, nobody thought that there was any point.'

'What if she didn't write them?' Martin continues, 'What if they were written by someone else?'

'Why would they be written by somebody else?' Helen says.

Max responds quickly, 'More importantly, why would they have been written by Joyce? And if she did write them, why did she not disguise her handwriting? If you were writing that kind of note, would you not want it to be anonymous?'

'This is one of the notes.' Helen is holding a scanned copy of a postcard sized note. On it are written the words, 'YOU ARE VERMIN. LEAVE NOW OR FACE THE CONSEQUENCES'.

Max looks at it and says, 'Are there others like this?'

'About nine or ten, I think. The vocabulary changes, but they are all written in capital letters and in the same handwriting: 'PERVERT', 'WEIRDO', 'YOU HAVE BEEN WARNED'; the sentiment remains the same.'

Martin looks at the scanned copy and says, 'You know, if I was going to write something like this, I would make sure that it couldn't be traced back to me.'

'Cutting out letters from magazines - like they do on the telly,' suggests Helen.

'Maybe,' Martin replies, 'but at the very least I would print them out from a computer. I would be terrified if I knew someone could get back at me. I wouldn't be able to sleep.'

'Exactly!' Max agrees, 'And another thing. Do you think, from what you know of Joyce, that she would have been the kind of person to write something like this?'

Both Martin and Helen shake their heads. 'We don't know this for certain,' says Martin, 'but from what we do know, it does seem unlikely.'

Max continues, 'So, for two reasons: firstly, that she didn't attempt to disguise her writing and secondly, because it appears to be so out of character for this frail, little old lady. Why would somebody who seems never to have harmed anyone, write such offensive and wounding stuff? And furthermore, write these notes to hurt someone whom she appears not to have encountered in anything other than a superficial way?

'There's something wrong here; something that's not been picked up - and that's where we'll start. Thanks for that.

'Martin! Make us all a cup of tea and then I'll get off to ForGiving. Helen, you will be able to use this morning to sort things out here - and get us logged into the system, and let's see if we can fix it so that we reduce all this paper work to a minimum. All these files must be on a drive somewhere, and we need have access to them as soon as possible.'

'We still have the original notes that were sent to Mickey?' says Martin.

'I would think so. We will have. They will have been filed away.' Helen looks to see if she has that information.

'Were they checked for prints or DNA?'

'I can't see from here,' she indicates the file, 'but I will find out, sir.'

'Thanks. I want them checked for DNA and dusted for prints immediately. How do I authorise that?'

'I will arrange it, sir,' Helen smiles as she closes her file. 'I'll let you know how things are progressing as soon as you get back to the office.'

'Call me on my mobile if anything exciting turns up - don't wait. That cup of tea, Martin? When you are ready!'

***

In ForGiving, Desmond, the shop manager is fussing around a display case when DI Wordsworth enters. He turns to see Max and says, 'Hi, are you chap who was looking for the binoculars? I've three or four pairs for you to look at - old ones, very collectable.'

Max shows his warrant card, 'No sir, I'm not a collector. I'm a police officer, DI Wordsworth. I am looking for the manager.'

'Wordsworth, eh?' smiles Desmond. 'Any relation to Will…?'

'No! Are you the manager?'

'For my sins, yes. How can I help you?'

'Is there somewhere we can talk privately?'

Desmond looks around, 'No, I'm sorry, there isn't. We don't have much space. We do have a room in the back - and I am supposed to have an office in there. But there are two ladies folding clothes, and my office doesn't have a door.'

'In that case,' replies Max, 'I want you to come to my office on Rydal Road and we can talk there.'

'The old police station? I'd heard it was up for sale.'

'Not yet. We are using it for our enquiries. When will you be free?'

'Today?'

'Yes, today. Now, if possible.'

Desmond puts on his busy face. 'Now is going to be difficult,' he says. 'These ladies aren't sufficiently *au fait* with the working of the till for me to be able to leave them.'

Max has had enough: 'This is not a request. I need to speak to you today. I'm going for a walk around the block. There are several other places I want to visit, and I will be back here in thirty minutes. I expect you to have made arrangements by then.'

He leaves the shop and walks down the hill. After about a hundred yards, he turns into a narrow lane - Lonsdale Street, walking slowly past what was Joyce's house. The notes that he has read mention that during the day this street is a rat-run, serving as a useful short cut for local drivers who wish to avoid the build-up of tourist traffic on the way into Ambleton. Cars are parked all along the full length of the street; it's no surprise that Forensics was unable to retrieve any material from outside the house.

He walks on, past a group of recently built 'town houses' - so small that the town they were built for was probably Lilliput - and he turns into the main road through Ambleton directly across from Alfred Hitchcock's, the local cinema and restaurant complex.

He then continues his walk up and around past the old Market Place, and back to the ForGiving shop. He has taken less than fifteen minutes, not the thirty that he had anticipated.

Desmond is waiting for him. 'It's all good, I've sent the ladies away, and we can close the shop for a few minutes. I don't want to hold up your investigations.'

'Thank you,' says Max, pleasantly surprised, 'I've walked past the house where Joyce was murdered. It's not far away, is it?'

'No. And that's why she liked working here. It was so convenient.'

'And you, how well did you get on with her? Did you ever visit her at home?'

'Visit her? No, I dropped her off at her home once or twice - she came with me to our warehouse in Kendal occasionally, and I used to bring her back. I don't think that I have ever been inside her home, but I got on with her quite well. She was very shy; she had been working here for a while before I started, and she was always polite and helpful to me. A gentle, pleasant woman.'

'Did you know that before she retired, she had been a store detective?'

'A what! A store detective - Joyce? I think you've got your wires crossed, Inspector. No, Joyce was far too meek to be a store detective. I always thought that she was something like a clerk - I never asked, but I assumed that she worked for the civil service, in one of the government agencies around Liverpool. They are the only people who can retire early on a full pension, aren't they?'

'No sir, she was a store detective - and very experienced. Did she mention anything to you? Had she noticed any suspicious activity?'

'What do you mean?' Desmond looks genuinely concerned. 'This is a charity shop. People don't steal from places like this.'

'You'd be surprised. In my experience, people steal from everywhere - all the time. Not only your customers, either. Have you noticed any items missing, any cash disappearing, any strange till reconciliations?'

'Not that I can think of,' replies Desmond. 'The till isn't always accurate, but that's invariably because of a mistake - a failure to account for the float, or an over-ring. I can't say that I have ever found any pattern of suspicious activity.

'A few weeks ago, a customer did come into the shop to try on some clothes and walked out wearing them - and without paying. That's about all.'

Max pursues his line, 'Did Joyce ever mention anything?'

'Never!' Desmond says this quite sharply. Maybe too sharply. He tries to soften the power of what he has just blurted out, 'Joyce and I got on very well together, so I would have been the first person that she spoke to, if she had any concerns. I am sure of that.'

Max is listening carefully, and he is also looking – 'hearing with his eyes', as the man said. On the communications skills course that he recently attended (not by choice, he was required to attend it!), the facilitator said that the words convey only seven percent of the total message. The tone of voice accounts for thirty-eight percent (it's not what you say, it's the way that you say it!), and your body language, the real give-away, accounts for fifty-five percent of the true meaning.

Although Desmond's words themselves when written down would appear entirely straightforward, his tone of voice, Max notes, is not congruent with those words.

Also, his body language, while not exactly twitchy, seems very defensive; the crossed arms and nose touching so obvious as to be almost a cliché. His eyes are furtive, and his face is flushed, and he seems to be trying to cut off Max's questions wherever he can, holding back something. Max tries another approach.

'Because of the situation, we will be requesting an immediate audit of ForGiving. Standard procedure: I am sure you understand.'

Max can't be certain, but he senses that something like a bolt of lightning has just zapped Desmond: the shop manager seems to freeze, then he looks into the distance, oblivious to Max, working something out in his head.

'I am surprised that there hasn't been one already,' Max continues, 'but I suppose your auditors are volunteers too.'

Desmond is working hard, regaining lost ground. He has recovered from whatever it was that froze his thinking. 'I am responsible for the management accounts, but for the yearly audit, someone comes from Head Office. That is a cost to us - comes off our bottom line. So, honestly, is it necessary? I think that I can give you all the answers that you need.'

Max goes along with this, 'Maybe you can. Although I am sure that your head office will want to know if anything has been going on.'

'Going on? What do you mean?'

'Something must have happened to precipitate the violence towards Joyce Todd.' Max wants to keep the initiative, 'We think that it could have had something to do with your shop. Joyce was well liked – but she was also an experienced floor walker, so there might have been people who held a grudge against her.'

'Her death might have been the result of something that had happened when she worked in Liverpool, but we don't think so. If you didn't know that Joyce was a store detective, it's possible that nobody else did, either. Our original suspect, Michael Hembrow, worked here too.'

'Mickey?'

'Yes, and that makes this shop the only common factor that we have, so far, apart from you, of course - and the other volunteers.'

'Me? I am just the manager here, I know nothing personal about Joyce - or why Mickey became involved. Although,' Desmond sees this as an opportunity, 'I am surprised that you didn't hang on to him a little longer.'

Max changes tack, not wishing to discuss the Mickey thing - yet. 'And the poison pen notes? Did you come across those?'

'You've lost me,' says Desmond. 'I don't know what you are talking about.'

'Did Mickey not confide in you? Did he not tell you about them?'

'No, Mickey has never confided anything in me. Why would he? He's a volunteer here, that's all. I try to be friendly to my staff, of course, but these people are not my friends.' The way he emphasizes the word 'friends' has Max interested.

Desmond continues, 'And, as I said, I think you made a mistake when you let him go. He was obviously guilty.'

'And how is that, exactly?' Max appears to be intrigued - the forward-lean, the focused body language emphasising his own interest - like they recommended on the course.

'It's obvious that Mickey is your man. He's the only person around here who could do something like this - he's ex-military, isn't he? He's got a huge inferiority complex too. He did it. You are wrong, and you know it. You are filling in your time to show - what is it, 'due diligence'?'

'I came to see you because we want to find the murderer of Miss Todd, Joyce - and we will. What about your relationship with her? Was she suspicious of you, perhaps?'

'Of course not!? Don't be ridiculous. Again, Joyce was a volunteer - and I saw her less frequently than I saw Mickey. She only came in on a Friday. This has nothing to do with me!'

Max stirs a little further, 'I believe that your wife works here also. Is that true?'

'And what has my wife got to do with this?'

'Probably nothing, but I will want to speak to her too – cover all the bases. If she could make herself available tomorrow, that would help me greatly. And,' he pauses before saying, 'I would like you both be prepared to undergo a DNA test.'

'That didn't happen last time!'

Max is quick to respond, 'Lots of things didn't happen last time, sir! The more I see of this investigation, the more I see that we jumped to hasty conclusions. So, if you have no objection?'

Desmond does not want to buckle under, 'I'm not sure about this, not sure at all. I think that I might well have an objection. I will have a word with my solicitor first.'

'Please do. I have asked you politely, and if after speaking to your solicitor, the answer is still no, we will compel you.'

'Compel?'

'Yes, you both could be material witnesses. Your solicitor might want to make something of this, but we would be justified in attempting to exclude you from our enquiries by testing you and your wife. Budgets are tight, as I am sure you realise.'

'Exclude us from your enquiries?'

'Of course, sir, what else? Will you come tomorrow – or later this afternoon, if you can manage it? My colleague DC Tomlinson will conduct the test. Thanks for your time. Bye.'

***

The next morning, DC Tomlinson and DI Wordsworth are enjoying their leisurely breakfast together. Martin has been trying the 'eat your hot food first' approach and is quite taken by it. His boss is reading the newspaper on his tablet and doesn't appear to want to be engaged in conversation.

The plan is to wander over to their offices soon and begin the task of DNA testing and fingerprinting. They have decided to test everyone who they think may have had any connection to the deceased, and particularly all the volunteers at ForGiving. Desmond and Donna did not appear yesterday, and DC Tomlinson has them at the top of his list.

As far as Max is concerned, this testing is so far the only tangible differentiator so far from the investigation that preceded theirs. While he is not entirely confident that it will solve his problems, he still expects things to move on a little from the stalemate that now exists.

The Desmond guy concerns him; he must know more than he is letting on. It's beyond belief that has had ~~bad~~ such a cursory relationship with his staff members. He is holding something back, and Max thinks that this conundrum needs solving quickly.

'Are we good to go, Martin?' He looks over at his DC who has rushed to pick up and answer his phone. Tell her you'll be home at the weekend. We've got to get moving.'

'It's Kendal police, sir. They have found a body!'

'Where?'

'Here, sir. Here in Ambleton. It's been there a long time, and apparently, it's not a pretty sight. They are on the scene now and want you to join them.

'They?'

'Uniform and CID, I think, sir.'

'They are sending a car. It's not far - on the outskirts of the village. The driver will be here in a few minutes.'

'Phone Helen, tell her where we are going, and why. Ask her to chase up anything that we have asked for so far, and that we'll be back in the office within the hour.'

Max notices the quizzical look on his young colleague, 'It's not our case, Martin. They only want to show us how efficient they are!'

And they do. There is a certain edginess to the atmosphere as DC Tomlinson and his boss are met at the door of the house. The body had been discovered when a utilities engineer called. There being no answer to his ringing the bell, he did what most of us would do in the circumstances - after noticing the car parked up next to the house - he peeked through the letterbox.

The stench that greeted him would make sure that he would think twice before peeking through another letterbox ever again.

Martin and Max, invited into the room by a DC with a wicked sense of humour, are only able to brave the putrefaction for a moment or two. Neither of them carries a handkerchief, so they must improvise by holding their jacket sleeves in front of their noses.

The duvet has been pulled back allowing the two police officers full benefit of the stench - another nice touch, thanks for that, thinks Max. They clearly see the remains of a man, definitely a man, dressed in men's pyjamas - lying on its side, curled, almost in a foetal position. The pyjamas are candy-striped and Winceyette, with a drawstring neatly tied. Martin notices the socks on the body with their brightly coloured heels and toes - matching, as well: another M&S man, he thinks.

As soon as they have proved their masculinity to the satisfaction of their observant colleagues, Max and Martin leave the house. Rather than go back to the office, at the same time as opening the car window and encouraging Martin to do the same, Max asks the driver to take them straight round to their hotel.

Each man acknowledges that a good long shower, with lots of lather, and probably more deodorant applied than is usual, will be more important than getting back to the office within the time they had promised.

***

Desmond and Donna are thinking; they have a lot to think about. Desmond seems to be the more concerned, 'He said that the DNA testing was to rule us out of their enquiries – I am worried that it will rule us in.'

'DNA? Testing for what?'

'Really, Donna! This *insouciance* is quite annoying at times.'

'Not as annoying as when you use big words like *insouciance*! What are they testing?'

'I assume they are testing to see if I - or you - you mostly, were involved in Joyce's death.'

Donna remains calm, 'I wasn't involved, was I?'

'You were involved in something! You came home that night with a big smile on your face and a couple of plastic refuse sacks full of stuff. The stuff disappeared quickly, but that smile lasted for days! And you said that we didn't have to worry about Joyce anymore! The next morning, she turns up dead!'

'That was nothing to do with me, Desmond - pure coincidence. I told you not to worry and I meant it. The police are simply doing their job.'

'I know you better than that! How can you behave so stupidly, and how can you tell me not to worry? You were involved in Joyce's death - somehow, I don't know how, but you were out that night, and when you came back, something had happened. It's impossible to draw any other conclusion.'

'Who else knows I was out that night?' Donna looks straight at her husband.

'I've no idea. How would I know?'

'Think! Who?'

'Nobody, as far as I know.'

'What were we doing?'

'We stayed in, didn't we?' Desmond remembers what he was told when Donna returned late that night. And another thing. They had sex that night - first time for a long time, and nothing since. Of course, he remembers.

'Exactly! That's what we did. We were at home all night, and the next day you went in to ForGiving and I joined you later. If you remember that, we'll be ok.'

'What happened! Tell me! Were you involved in Joyce's death? DNA testing, Donna - if you were, they'll probably find out.'

'How many times? You know already. I was - otherwise occupied - nothing to do with Joyce. And what I did was because I was so angry with you. I was thinking of leaving you - and I was ready to go. I told you that I had some options, and I had. Two, in fact.'

'Two options?'

'Two alternatives to staying here with you. You had angered me so much over the weekend, remember? That night, as we sat in the car dithering about Joyce, I decided to explore the - possibility: I decided that if I was going to leave you, now would be the time. I knew that 'Option Two', that is what I called him - Option Two was available, so I decided to test him out.'

'Test him out?' Desmond's imagination goes into overdrive.

'Yes, with a view to leaving you. Finding out what it might be like - to be with someone else. I was very confused, Desmond. I wanted to leave you, I really wanted to get away from you!'

'But you came back.'

'I did - of course, I did.'

'What was in those bags? You brought two black bags back to the house, and then they disappeared. What was in them?'

'Nothing! Some clothes.'

'Clothes?'

'Yes, clothes - two or three dresses, some skirts and an old fur coat. That was the pretext for his meeting me - and for me being prepared to see him. He said that he had some of his wife's clothes that could go to ForGiving. But he wanted me to look at them first. So, when I left you, and went over the road to Alfred's, I called him. He was round in a flash - very keen!'

'We chatted in his car, and I explained your problem with Joyce.'

'You did what?'

'Not too much detail, but I had to, darling. I had to! I said that yes, I had decided to leave you, and that I was prepared to think about moving in with him. But I couldn't leave you to face the horrors of Joyce. You needed my support.

'He then asked me what he could do to prove himself to me. You weren't going to do anything, so I suggested that he have a word with Joyce - have a word with her, that's all - to see if she would think again. I told him that she had a sheaf of price tags somewhere in the house, and we simply had to get them. I gave him the plastic bag I was carrying so that he would have something to put the tickets in, and I left him to it.'

'Did you go into Joyce's house?'

'Of course not! I stayed in his car around the back of Alfred's. Nobody came past; nobody saw me.'

'Then he must have killed Joyce? Christ almighty! Who the hell is he?'

'I didn't think that you could handle that information then, and I still don't. I won't tell you, Desmond. All you need to know is that on the night, we talked - that's all we did, we talked. He brought me the price tags and then gave me the clothes that I brought home when he dropped me off.

'I had already decided that I didn't want to see him again, so I made sure that there was no further excuse for us to meet. The clothes went into ForGiving.'

'When?'

'The next week. There were lots of bags that week, you remember?'

Desmond is not sure, but that is not what is at the forefront of his mind now. His mind is racing: Donna was going to leave him, was she?

'You went to this 'Option Two' bloke for some of his wife's things?'

'His dead wife's things: that was the excuse.'

'And you were going to leave me for him? And there was an 'Option One' too, I suppose?'

'Desmond let's get this straight. At that moment, I was going to leave you for anyone - anyone at all!'

'Where is he now, this 'Option Two'?'

'I don't know, darling. Honestly, I don't know. I have been dreading him coming into the shop, but that night was the last time I saw him. He had made me all sorts of promises, but I haven't heard from him since.'

And 'Option One?' Is he still around?'

'He was never in my thoughts; that was all in his head, not mine. And as for Option Two, he knows that he could never replace you - I set him straight on that as soon as I realised the mistake that I had made.

'Nobody can replace you, Desmond. It was never going to happen. Let me tell you something: even when I had convinced myself that I truly wanted to leave - I couldn't. Why? Because I need you with me. I know that now. We both know that now.'

And she moves towards her husband and into his waiting arms.

Desmond takes her, holds her tightly as she begins to cry a little. This has been quite a moving scene, and the tears are real.

He listens to her as she sniffles into his shoulder. She is a lying little bitch, of course, but if their well-planned lies can save her, and by extension, him, he will have to go along with it.

There is still the matter of their empty bank account to broach with her. Desmond has partly retrieved the situation through skimming a little more from each day's takings than he would realistically consider sensible, and he has been strict with himself - staying away from the sparkly magic of the roulette wheel.

However, the thought of an imminent audit at ForGiving does make him clench, even though he knows that their stock control system is so lax that it will be difficult for anyone to prove any fraud, now that those price tags have disappeared.

Should he strike while this particular iron is still quite warm and confess all to Donna, or should he wait? He decides to wait. 'Something will turn up', as a fictional character, in many ways not unlike Desmond, once said.

***

Max and Helen are listening to Martin, DC Tomlinson, as he reports on his work over the last couple of days.

'There are about thirty people who are known to have had direct contact with Joyce at ForGiving. Most of them are volunteers, past and present. The list includes the manager and his wife, Desmond and Donna Blain.'

'Past and present?' says Helen.

'Not dead 'past', but 'former' past - ex volunteers. It appears that the current manager's style does not suit some of them. They have stopped volunteering, about eight or so in this list - I've underlined their names - but they still pop in and out of the shop, mostly when Desmond is not there.'

'And he's not there quite often,' adds Max.

'Yes, sir, but to be fair, it is only a part time job.   Notionally fifteen hours a week.'

'I stand corrected, Martin. Carry on.'

'I have obtained fingerprints and DNA samples from twenty-two people, including the manager and his wife. If there are any matches with people on our database, those results will be with us today or tomorrow.'

'I'd be surprised if any of them has a criminal record,' says Helen.

'Mickey has! That's what got us into this mess,' says Max quickly.

'Forensics is going to take a little longer. But the shop and Joyce's house have been dusted already.'

Max looks up at his DC, 'You know that death, earlier this week? Is it suspicious in any way?'

Helen answers, 'CID attended, as you know. It seems that it was a lonely old man who died in his sleep. Tucked up tight, wearing his pyjamas. No signs of a struggle. Neighbours say that they never saw him. Nobody had visited the house for weeks.'

'Post-mortem?'

Helen looks at her screen, 'It's not a suspicious death, and there are no next of kin, sir.'

'So, no post mortem?'

'I'm not sure, sir. I don't think that one has been carried out yet.'

'Do we know when the guy died?'

'Three to four weeks ago, sir, Best guess.'

'Helen,' Max is quite animated. He stands up and puts his phone into his pocket. 'Find out who this person was, include him in the DNA and fingerprint exercise, if possible, and let's see if we can't get a post-mortem too. He's not been cremated yet, has he?'

'I don't think so, sir, no.'

'C'mon Martin, we are going to do some sleuthing while Helen sorts out all the procedural stuff. Is that ok. Helen?'

'Certainly sir!'

'Good, and when we return, DC Tomlinson here will bring you a cake.'

'If I can choose, sir, it would be a custard tart.'

Martin smiles at Helen and says, 'Your wish is my command! See you later!'

***

Ambleton is a delightfully small town; more a village, with a total population of only about three thousand. The drive to where the death had been discovered takes only five minutes as the two police officers make their way out of the village via Rydal Road and back into Under Loughrigg via Pelter Bridge.

As Max and Martin pull up to the door, a PCSO has just locked up and is putting the keys in her pocket.

Martin shows his warrant card and introduces his boss. 'Will you open up for us again? We want to take a closer look at the scene.'

'Certainly sir. I'll have to ok it with Control, give me a moment.' And she does so. Two minutes later, Max and Martin have opened the front door and they start looking around the house.

'Anything?' Max is the first to ask.

'I don't think so, sir, no - it's very tidy though, isn't it?'

'Amazingly tidy for a single man, don't you agree? A - fastidious man? A very tidy, fastidious man, but a man who sleeps with his socks on!'

'Sir?'

'He slept with his socks on, remember? Would such a man sleep with his socks on?'

'I don't know.'

'Well I do! My mother caught me once - sleeping with my socks on, and she said did I think I was a tramp, and it was no wonder that my bedroom was as filthy as it was - because people who slept with their socks on were 'moral degenerates'!

'I wasn't a moral degenerate - I was a fifteen-year-old boy. I have never forgotten how angry she was over that. Since then, I've never slept with my socks on. Have you?'

Martin isn't sure, and he says so. What he does say is, 'It's not a lot to be going on sir. I mean, if we think it's suspicious.'

'But look here!' They are in the kitchen now and Max has opened the top drawer. The cutlery is laid out with military precision: everything in exactly the right place. In the glass-fronted wall cupboards, all glasses, cups and saucers, and all the plates and bowls that can be seen are perfectly positioned.

'This,' says Max, 'settles it for me.' He points to the interior of the saucepan cupboard. The pans, the frying pans; all the cookware is, once again, lined up as in a display at the Ideal Home exhibition.

'I can't believe that a man who is this particular about every one of his possessions would wear his socks in bed. I don't buy it - it's not even winter!'

He takes his phone out of his shirt pocket and speed dials the office. Helen answers. 'Helen, this is a suspicious death, push for that post mortem. It's going to be important. If I need to sign anything, make sure it is ready for me when I return to the office. We'll probably be an hour or so; DI Tomlinson and I are popping to ForGiving again.

'And Helen, there was a third death, wasn't there? That was also connected to ForGiving, wasn't it? Yes, the guy who died in his gym at home? Arrange for me to see any paperwork regarding that too. And let me know the connection with ForGiving - who the volunteer is. Ok! Thanks, Helen.'

***

Mickey is serving behind the till. He has been back on his regular shift at ForGiving for a while now, and so far, the only kind of unpleasantness he has experienced has been from Donna and Desmond - Desmond particularly, who has taken to ignoring him. The other volunteers whom he has met all seem to be supportive. It may be that they say things differently behind his back, but as that has happened all his life, he is impervious to it.

But he is not impervious to the idea of a couple of plain clothes police officers coming through the door, and when they do, Mickey nearly has a heart attack.

'You must be Michael Hembrow,' says Max smiling. 'I'm DI Wordsworth and this is DC Tomlinson. I'd like a word - relax - it's only a word. We haven't come to arrest you. We'd like your help.'

Mickey takes a deep breath and tries to calm himself down. Even though there are no customers in the shop to see his shame, he knows that his face is flushed bright red and if anybody looks guilty at this moment - it wouldn't take a Sherlock Holmes to make the deduction!

Max continues: 'I want to ask you a few questions. Is there anybody in the back of the shop?'

At that moment, Monica walks through from the back.   Monica is good at being brisk and efficient. 'Is anything the matter, Mickey? May I help you gentlemen?'

Max introduces himself and his DC, and asks if they might go into the back room of the shop while Monica looks after the till - or would she prefer it if the shop was closed? No, she is quite happy to take over from Mickey, and the two of them change places. Max can't help but notice that there is something of an atmosphere between the two volunteers. Even though Mickey was released without charge, there has evidently been some collateral damage to his relationships here.

In the back room, all three men sit, and Max begins, 'I'm interested to know a little more about these notes - the notes that you think Joyce was writing.'

'What do you want to know?'

'You say that they were aimed at you. How do you know that? Could they have been intended for someone else?'

'I wondered that myself,' replies Mickey, 'at first. It had to be a mistake. But no, they were aimed at me. I often leave some things here at the shop, not much, but occasionally a book, or some cans of dog food in a bag. I don't drive, so if there is too much for me to carry, I leave some stuff here - and pick it up next time I am in the shop.

'The notes were always in my things - in the leaves of a book, in my pockets, under or in a bag of dog food. So, I stopped leaving anything overnight, but it still continued. For a while, I was also the person who was in charge of sorting the menswear - suits, jackets, trousers and so on. Sometimes I'd find a note in there too - in a pocket - or pinned to the lapel of a jacket. So, I know that they were put there for me to find.'

Martin interrupts, 'And these notes, you were sure that they came from Joyce?'

'They had to be from her, didn't they? I found it hard to believe because she seemed such a pleasant woman.   Always smiling - but I compared price tags that I know she had written to some of the notes I received, and they were definitely written by her.'

'But you thought that it was out of character - for her?'

'Totally! I was amazed, and shocked. I was going to confront her, but then, well, you know what I mean...' And the sentence tails off.

Max says, 'Mickey, if I was going to write something offensive and send it to you, do you think that I would disguise my writing in some way?'

Mickey looks at the older police officer, 'I thought that too. I did. But the notes are so obviously Joyce's.'

'So it would seem. Thanks for that, Mickey,' says Max. 'Please keep this to yourself for now. That would help.'

As they are leaving the shop, Max notices Monica. She is standing by the till and looking worried. He smiles at her and says. 'please don't worry about your colleague, madam. Mickey was a mistake on our part. We are trying to set things right: he's not a suspect.'

***

Back at Rydal Road, Helen is waiting for Max and Martin. 'I have the file on the third death, sir.'

'The head teacher?'

'Yes, sir. Officially it is an accidental death. He and his family had built a small exercise room in the basement of their house. He was a weightlifter - he'd done this for years - and the accident apparently occurred while he was bench-pressing.' She points to the file that she has created for Max, 'One hundred and thirty kilos - some weight! It says here that he must have failed to

114

get the weights back up on their stand. The weights slipped and pinioned him to the bench, choking him.'

'The connection with ForGiving?'

'The wife, Julia. She is a volunteer at the shop, has been for some time. She was out jogging when this happened. She came back to find him dead, called the police and waited.'

'We know that do we?'

'Yes, sir. The report says that she was able to prove it.'

'Does this woman, Julia, have any known connection other than the volunteering one?'

'No sir, none. She lives quite a long way away, so shall I ask here to come and see you?'

Martin asks, 'Any suspicious circumstances?'

Max is glancing at the file, 'They are all suspicious circumstances, aren't they?'

'I suppose so, sir, but this one is not connected to Ambleton, and Joyce, is it?'

'God knows! I don't, that's for certain. This recent death. The one we attended today. Any connection with ForGiving?'

'Not that we know of, sir.'

'So, let me sum up.' Max folds his arms and stares at the floor as he says, 'Sitrep, as they say - one murder investigation badly screwed up; two other deaths, one violent, one weird. They'll want an interim report from me tomorrow. Is that what I am going to have to say?'

Helen is not comfortable with the way that Max has described the situation. 'It's not as bad as that, sir. The death of the head teacher is probably unconnected to Ambleton - even though the victim's wife worked at ForGiving.'

'Well, that's all right, then!' says Max in his best 'don't you worry your pretty little head about it' voice. 'I'm going for a pint. Coming, Martin?'

'No sir, I want to clear off this stuff first. Fresh head for the morning.'

'As you wish,' says Max, catching both Martin's eye and that of Helen in turn. 'Probably see you later.'

A strangulated 'Yes, sir,' is the only reply that Martin can offer - his throat seems strangely constricted.

After Max has left to walk across the road and up the hill to the Golden Rule pub, Helen says, 'It's all right, Martin. I can tidy up if you want to go and join Max.'

He looks at her, not quite sure how to phrase it, but tries anyway, 'If you don't mind, I'd rather be here - with you.'

'Oh. Ok. I'd like that,' she replies. And she gives him the smile that she has been storing up for this very moment.

***

The silence at breakfast the next morning is palpable. Max and Martin eat at the same table, both starting with the hot food first. There has been a cursory

'Good Morning', but nothing else. When Martin, having finished his breakfast, leaves to make his now customary phone call to his girlfriend, neither man acknowledges the other. Something of a frost has set in.

They both know why, but neither knows what to do with the new elephant in their room, and their five-minute walk to Rydal Road continues in an embarrassing silence.

Helen is already in the office when the two police officers arrive. She too seems similarly less comfortable with the atmosphere than before. There is a nervousness about her which is expressed by her spilling one of the cups of coffee she has been making for her colleagues. She saw the two men coming along the road past the Bridge House and put the kettle on. She manages to grab a paper towel and wipe up the mess before her colleagues come in to the office.

All fingers and thumbs, she has been awake since about six o'clock and is dreading this moment. All she said to Max about her being professional comes back to her. Ha! Her sudden febrile state has been kicked off by the beginning of a new and powerful relationship with Martin, and nobody in the equation has thought it through. Nothing has changed, but *everything* has changed.

The spikiness continues from the entrance of the two men and into their first exchanges. Super-polite, deferential and ridiculous at the same time.

'So, Helen, where do we go from here?' Max's first question of the morning would have been answered in a perfectly sensible and logical way - yesterday. But today? What is the sub-text, is there a sub-text? Now that there is a need to go *somewhere* both in the case and in this new and suddenly important relationship with Martin. Helen is at a loss what to say.

Max's next comment doesn't help much either; it's almost as if he is trying to humiliate her. He follows his first question with, 'You were going to tidy away a few things yesterday, both of you. Did that tidying away bring any fresh insights that I should know about?' He then makes things slightly easier, but only slightly, by adding, 'About the case?'

Martin realises - it was obvious - but that is now confirmed. Max knows that he and Helen were together last night, and that was the purpose in his staying behind with her.

'The telephone numbers, sir.'

'Telephone numbers?'

Martin's train of thought is broken by Helen who answers the question, 'Yes, sir. It was Martin's idea - DC Tomlinson, sir. We looked at Joyce's call lists. There were not many, but on the night she was killed, she took a call quite late in the evening, at 2237.'

'Yes, that was in the report. We know about that.'

'We do sir; it was from a call box here in Ambleton.

'Do we know who made the call yet? Any CCTV?'

'No, we don't know that. There is no CCTV in the area.'

'So why are you mentioning it now?' Max's frustration at how the morning is going is displaced by the forceful way that he slumps into his chair. 'Tell me something new!'

There is a pause; Helen fills it. 'We do have something more important to tell you sir. Have you mentioned it yet, Martin?'

Still thinking of mixed messages, Martin is slow on the uptake, but then realises that he is to follow on from Helen's information - Get a grip man, he tells his inner self.

'I didn't want to spoil your breakfast this morning and thought it better if we were all together so that we could work out what to do.'

'What's the matter with you? What do you have to say?'

'It was just a punt, sir, something that Helen and I decided - almost at the same time.'

'Exactly at the same time! It was eerie!'

'Well,' Martin continues. 'Helen and I went through the time sequence of Joyce's murder, and we know that she received a telephone call at 2237.'

'We've been through that.'

'Yes - bear with us, sir - but because another body was discovered yesterday, Darren Melling's, and what with all the uncertainty, I decided - we decided - to pull up his phone records too.'

'And?'

'He also received a call that night - three hours earlier, and from the same phone box!'

'Yes, sir,' continues Helen. 'The first call, the one we already knew about, was one of the reasons that ruled the original suspect out. Michael Hembrow could not have made it. But this second call from the same box, and to someone who seems to have died at about the same time...'

'Is more than a coincidence!' Max completes the sentence. 'This is a result - deserving of another cup of coffee - which I will make!'

Max stands, moves to the kettle, fills it, switches it on and then turns to his colleagues.

'Well done, both of you. If there is a connection between these two deaths, this will change everything.

'We'll also have more leverage to get a proper PM on the man's body - Darren, wasn't it?'

'Yes, sir,' replies Martin. 'Darren Melling. There is a definite connection. Somehow these cases are linked.'

Max has more to say, but his tone is different, more conciliatory, 'I also feel that I should apologise to both of you as well. I have been on the wrong track entirely. I thought that you two had...'

'We had sir,' Helen breaks in, 'I mean, we haven't ... yet.' She blushes, looks at Martin and then adds, 'Your instincts were right, sir. In one way I'm sorry, but in another way, not. I made the best decision I ever made in my life last night.'

'Me too, sir. If this is an embarrassment, I apologise, but I feel the same way.' Martin and Helen are standing together, both looking in expectation at their boss.

Martin continues, 'I know it's difficult, and if you wish, I'm happy to be pulled off the case. But Helen and I ...' His voice trails off as Max says, 'I'm surprised that it's taken you so long!'

Max smiles, 'It was obvious from the first time you met, so I've nothing to say on the matter, only that I hope you've thought all this through.' And with a long look directed at Martin, he says, 'I'm sure that you know what I mean.'

'Yes, sir,' Martin replies.

'So, let us get on. Let's find a murderer. While we are waiting for forensics to do their work, we should begin to collate our own results so far. You two will still be able to work together, won't you?'

Martin is the first to reply. 'I think we'd be happy to, sir.'

'I thought so - this is the bit I hate the most, the paperwork, the reports and all the covering of all the bases that is so frustrating. Give me the file on that poor guy who choked himself with his weightlifting gear. I want to satisfy myself that it was an accident.'

'Or a suicide.' Max turns and looks at Martin who has made the interjection, and replies, 'Yes, the accidental death conclusion was possibly expedient - I'm thinking it might well have been sympathetic towards the family. Is that what you are saying, Martin?'

'I think so, sir, yes. And if that's what they have decided, we should leave it at that. After all, the man is dead - and there is nothing that we have found to link his death to our murders. There are court cases coming up soon, and although he is not going to be appearing, I imagine he will still have a role to play at the trial. That will be difficult for his family.

'And given the bad publicity that would be generated, I think that in this instance we should be very careful - before we rock this boat.'

'Yup, probably right. I don't see a link except for the fact that the wife worked at ForGiving. If the DNA profiles throw up anything, or her fingerprints suddenly start to play a role, we need to be prepared. But otherwise, I will recommend that we focus on Joyce Todd and Darren Melling.'

***

Three days later, Helen opens her computer at the Rydal Road office and two new files are waiting for her. More than twenty people have been fingerprinted, and all have had their DNA taken without complaint. Such a quick turnaround of this material speaks volumes for the interest that is being taken in this case, and its priority over so many other demanding causes.

Even Desmond and his wife, Donna have volunteered their samples, the conversation with Desmond's solicitor not having proved necessary after all.

Immediately, Helen forwards the material on to her two police colleagues. They will pick it up on their smartphones, or it will be on their desktops when they log in. This is going to be an important day. Even though she has spent the last two evenings with Martin, and the *coup de foudre* that threw them together is still working its magic, she knows how important it is going to be for them both to be completely professional in their handling of the details of this case.

They are making new plans every day; Martin has extricated himself - so he believes - from a cloying relationship in Preston and is now working on getting a transfer up to Cumbria constabulary as soon as possible.

The current work must go on, and after Martin and Max arrive to start the new day, there is not a sign of anything other than an entirely professional process taking place. They are both aware of the sensitivity of all this, particularly aware of the need to keep Max on side. They have great respect for him and are working hard so as not to embarrass him.

After a few minutes of desultory conversation, coffee-based, mostly, Helen asks if they have read the material that she has sent on to them.

They have received it, so the system works, but neither has read it. Max explains that he hates reading anything on the tiny iPhone screen. Martin agrees, and as he catches Helen's eye, the memories of last night come flooding back. Nevertheless, they must plough on.

All three look at their computer screens and begin to access the forensic reports that have come in.

Firstly, they see that the PMs of both Joyce Todd and Darren Melling have been completed. While the cause of death is obvious in the case of Joyce, the deterioration of Darren's body in the weeks up to is discovery, make it impossible to be sure. It is Helen who notices the first of the correlations.

'Here sir. Look at this. Two samples: one found at Joyce's house, the other found at Darren's. The samples belong to the same person.'

'Found at Darren's? So, he's connected?'

'Yes, sir. No doubt. One sample is from a paper tissue.' Helen finds it difficult to formulate the right words, 'Nose discharge, sir.'

'Technical term, snot?'

'Yes, sir. Snot. That was found at Joyce's house – on the floor by the sofa and, but under the body. Maybe dropped during the struggle?'

'Possibly. Was it obvious?'

'The photos of the scene do show it. There were also one or two other pieces of paper on the floor - price tags - from the ForGiving shop.'

'And what did we find at Darren's house?'

'A pubic hair, sir.'

'One?''

'Yes, sir.' She's not blushing, but Helen is uncomfortable about sharing this piece of information. 'A single pubic hair - in his mouth, sir. It was found under his tongue.'

It's not an embarrassed silence, but nevertheless, a silence ensues. Max, Martin and Helen are all processing the news, each in their own way.

'Darren had a sexual encounter with the person who killed Joyce?'

'We think so,' Martin continues, 'And maybe that same person was involved in Darren's death in some way.'

'His death a murder too?' Max is scrolling through the information on his screen as he suggests this. Martin takes him up on it.

'You saw Darren - you even mentioned that he was wearing socks in bed.'

'Yes,' Max replies, 'but it was the overall neatness of everything - the perfection of each object, perfectly placed, and it seemed so incongruous that he would go to sleep wearing his socks.'

'Yes,' adds Helen, 'and because of that comment, the pathologist has looked carefully at those socks and, of course, Darren's ankles.

'He can't be sure, but he thinks that his ankles could have been restrained in some way, and that the socks could have been put on his feet to hide the restraint marks - if that's what they were.'

Even though this was his concern, Max is not convinced: 'Not much to go on.'

'No sir. But look at page three. The report says that Darren's room - the room where his body was found - had been 'diligently cleaned'. No other forensic evidence was found. If there was sexual activity in that room, all signs of it were cleared away - diligently, sir.'

Max asks, 'Is that possible? I mean is it possible to clear away all forensic evidence? I wouldn't have thought so. There has to be something left.'

Martin chips in, 'Not always. That was one of the first things we were told on the Forensics element of my degree. Here, somebody cleaned the scene thoroughly. Not only that, it's possible that some items were removed from the house - bedsheets and so on - replaced by new, clean bedlinen. The pyjamas he was wearing could have been put on afterwards.

He continues, 'Just saying, but if he had been involved in some sexual activity, and was being restrained; we're probably talking handcuffs cuffs here, he wouldn't be wearing his pyjamas, would he? I know I wouldn't!'

'That's good to know,' says Max smiling as he watches his colleague's face turn crimson with embarrassment. In present company, that was a step too far. Helen, he notices, is busy avoiding any chance of being drawn into the conversation, but there is definitely some blushing going on there too.

Her gambit is to move things into another direction. 'We do have a link, sir.'

'The link?'

'Yes, the link between the two deaths. Forensics has established that at least one person was at both sites - at some time. We can work with that information.'

'We can. Let's see who this mystery person is.' He flicks through the report, frustrated by the language, 'I wish they'd make these things clearer. Doctors talking to doctors doesn't make good reading for plods like me.'

'Have a look at page five sir - at the bottom.'

And he does.

***

The forensic evidence that has been found at both sites causes some consternation, and far from being a relatively easy matter, it throws up a few embarrassing complications.

Max decides that the best way to deal with it is to bring the people concerned in for questioning, rather than make the move that he needs to make in too heavy-handed a manner. The evidence is overwhelming in one sense, extremely surprising in another and completely bewildering however it is stacked.

He must get it right: he now knows who the murderer is, but if he gets it wrong, although it will be the first time for him, many senior members of the Force would have difficulty in surviving a second debacle.

His focus is on the 'management team' at ForGiving, and it is here where the answers are to be found.

Max has asked both Desmond and Donna Blain to come in, and they dutifully arrive at Rydal Road exactly on time. Max greets them, introduces them to Martin and begins the interview. Helen has been asked to collect some supplementary information from the Forensics lab in Lancaster, and so it falls to Martin to offer the social niceties to the two, slightly nervous guests.

'Tea? Coffee? Water?'

'Nothing, thank you. Let's get this over with so that we can get back to work. We have had to shut the shop as there is only one volunteer working this afternoon.' Desmond is not in one of his more convivial moods.

Max takes over, 'As you know, we have been investigating the murder of Ms Joyce Todd. Our enquiries have led us to another death, one which came to our notice a couple of days ago, but which probably happened around the time that Ms Todd was killed. We are not sure about the exact time of death, but we are treating the two cases as linked, and this second case as suspicious. Did either of you ever meet a Mr Darren Melling?'

Desmond, geared up to do the answering, charges in with, 'Darren Melling? Never heard of him!' He turns to his wife. 'What about you, pet? Does it strike a bell?'

'No,' Donna replies, choosing not to elaborate. Desmond continues, 'Was this person the death that you are referring to?'

'Yes, sir. It is. Mr Melling's body was found at his house at Under Loughrigg two days ago. He had been dead for some time, and we now believe that he was murdered.'

'And why are you asking us about someone that we have never met?'

'I wanted to make sure that you hadn't met him, sir. To confirm: you have never met Mr Darren Melling?'

'No - I, that is we, have never met him. I'm telling you now, and my wife told you the same thing a moment ago.'

'Thank you. I now would like to interview you both, but separately. If this is acceptable, we will continue. One of you will leave the room. You may sit outside, and if you wish, DC Tomlinson will rustle up a cup of something for you.

'However, either or both of you may wish to have a solicitor present during these interviews. If so, I will caution you now, and we will set an appointment for the further interviews. Which is it to be?'

Desmond looks towards his wife and decides for them both. 'Since we are here, we might as well carry on.'

'Is that acceptable to you, Mrs Blain?' Max wants to – needs to - get the balance right.

'If it's all right with my husband, then it is all right with me,' is Donna's brief reply.

Max looks at this woman sitting in front of him, barely acknowledging her husband as he leaves the room. She is attractive, no doubt about that. Obviously, she is slightly older than the range in which Max's preferences centre, but nevertheless he can see why she might be interesting to men of a certain age. She is looking at him now, her eyes worth a second look and her demeanour one of complete self-possession.

Max begins, 'This is proving to be a difficult case for all of us, and I am sorry to have to drag you here.'

'No, I understand. Believe me, I would like things to get back to normal as soon as possible.'

'And you believe they can?'

'Can what?'

'Get back to normal? Personally, I don't see how. This has changed the lives of so many people. Victims, and their families.'

Donna interrupts, 'Joyce didn't have any family, did she?'

'No immediate family, true. But her life was centred around ForGiving, wasn't it? There are people there who have been damaged by her death - Mickey, for one.

'He's having to deal with the fact that he was arrested and kept in a cell. He tells me that people see him differently now. And there are others. Tell me about Desmond, please.'

The speed at which Max segues into her own life and that of her husband catches Donna a little off guard, but she takes a breath and says, 'What do you want to know?'

'One of the insights that Mickey shared with us was that he didn't feel confident voicing his concerns about Joyce Todd with your husband. Mickey believed that Joyce had been sending him poison pen letters but couldn't talk about this to him; he found him cold, distant. And after his arrest, it was Desmond, and to some extent you, who made Mickey feel particularly embarrassed. Would you agree?'

'How would I know what Mickey thinks, and what has this to do with Joyce?'

'Two days ago, the body of a man called Darren Melling was found at his house in Under Loughrigg. We believe that he was murdered on or around the time of Joyce's death. Darren Melling was a regular customer at ForGiving, wasn't he?'

'No idea. I rarely get to know the names of the customers at ForGiving.'

'But he always sought you out, didn't he? Always wanted to chat to you. That's what one of your volunteers has told DC Tomlinson.'

'Ah, yes. Him. I know who you are talking about. I didn't know that was his name. Why do you think that he was murdered?'

'I asked both of you about this person, and you both denied knowing him.'

Donna pauses before she quietly says, 'Desmond asked me to.'

'Do you do everything that Desmond asks you to?'

'Certainly not! He said that this was important.'

'We now have specific evidence, Mrs Blain, and I will make that clear soon. But before I do, can you remember where you were on the night that Joyce was murdered?'

'I was at home all evening.'

'With your husband?'

'Yes, I think so,'

'All evening?'

'I think so.'

'Are you sure?'

'Here's the thing. I assume so, but I have to say, Inspector, I am not sure. No, I can't be sure, and I am sorry that I can't be more helpful.'

'Why is that?'

'As I remember, we were not talking to each other at that time. I had got into a strop, and so I had been ignoring him - staying in my own room.'

'Do you not share a bedroom?'

'What has that got to do with you?'

'I have to ask you - this could be quite important.'

'Desmond and I have not 'shared a bedroom' for many years. Please don't press me on that. I don't want to talk about it.'

'I am a police officer, madam. I'll press where I need to press. Are you saying that on the night Joyce died, Desmond might not have been with you?'

'I'm pretty sure he was at home; I can't be exactly sure. He may have gone out - he often did - does go out.'

'Where does he go?'

'Ha! Who knows? I certainly don't!'

Max is alerted by this nuance. He wants to pursue tit further - yes, they are going round in circles, but this conversation is certainly turning out differently from the way that he had expected.

Donna clarifies things, 'You know that you said that this man, Darren Melling, came into ForGiving to see me?'

'Yes.'

'Well, he did come in to see me, and he did make a big thing about it, but that was for show.'

'For show?'

'Yes, it wasn't me that he was interested in.'

'No?'

'You now have your answer.'

'To what?'

'To the question asking if Desmond and I share a bedroom. We don't, and that is the reason why.'

'Darren is the reason why?'

'Ha! If only! No, Darren is not *the* reason why - not the *only* reason. Darren is *one* of the reasons why. One of the many reasons why. Darren is - was originally from Blackpool, wasn't he? Des... my husband will have met Darren there - it's one of his favourite haunts.'

'So, you think that Desmond knew Darren Melling?'

'Of course, he knew him. He came into the shop once or twice a week. He pretended that I was the one he was looking for, so that the volunteers had something to gossip about. He was very discreet, but they have - signals - don't they?'

'Who?'

'That kind of man. They recognise each other.'

'That kind of man? Oh, I see. And you were all right with this?'

'With Desmond and his - friends? 'All right' is probably not correct, but 'accepting' certainly. I do still love him, Inspector; I always have loved him. But a little while after we were married, a year or so after, I found out about his true - preferences.'

'And you stayed with him?'

'It's complicated. I suppose that I should have left him, but it had its advantages too.'

'Advantages?'

'I did not expect to be talking about this, you know.'

'I know, but you are being helpful. You mentioned that Desmond's 'preferences' had certain advantages for you. What were they?'

'He had his needs met elsewhere.'

'And was that not difficult for you?'

'No, Not at all. Not in the slightest.' She looks at Martin and then back at Max. Both men are wondering what she might say next.

'This might surprise you, Inspector, but put simply, I have never enjoyed physical intimacy - the sexual side of marriage. I don't like sex. In fact, I hate it. I have no interest at all.'

'Why is that?'

'Oh, there were reasons - I had a difficult time as a child, and of course, people never talked about that kind of thing. But it put me off. I couldn't wait to get out and forget everything.

'I married Desmond when I was young - on my sixteenth birthday, and I married to escape my family.

'To begin with, I tried to be a devoted wife, and I even tried to make the sex thing work. Desmond was my first real relationship, and I did like living with him - I always have. I am still in love with him, but ours was never a truly sexual relationship.

'Maybe that's why it has lasted so long. The physical part of our life petered out quite quickly, and I never wanted children. Desmond always had a feminine side, you will have noticed it yourselves. So, when he started to develop his 'interests', I let him. He's wasn't doing anything illegal as far as I know. A bit unsavoury, perhaps, but I let him get on with it. I was quite surprised to find that it was still going on - he's not a young man, after all.'

'Do you think that he met Darren Melling that evening?'

'I honestly have no idea. I can't remember, but I doubt it. However, I will say one thing, Inspector. If this Darren Melling was killed, it would not have been Desmond who killed him. He is a gentle person at heart, and I know that he could not do that kind of thing.'

'What I would like you to do, Mrs Blain, is put what you have told me in the form of a statement. DC Tomlinson here has been taking notes, and he will help you.'

'And what is going to happen?'

'I am grateful to you for answering my questions. You are helping us to understand the context a little more. And while we are completing your statement, I will be speaking to your husband.'

'You mentioned that you had some evidence?'

'Yes, madam, we do.'

'What is it, this evidence?'

'I can't tell you. What I can say is that so far it seems consistent with our thinking. But it is delicate, and I want to be quite sure of my ground before I divulge anything to a third party.'

'And that's me? I'm a third party, am I?'

'In these circumstances, yes you are. But you have been very helpful. Let's get on with that statement, shall we? Would you like a coffee or a tea?'

'I'll have a tea, please. No milk, no sugar.'

'That's easy enough. DC Tomlinson, would you take a statement from Mrs Blain - and make her a cup of tea?'

'Call me Donna, please!'

'I think Mrs Blain is more appropriate now. This shouldn't take long.'

***

While Donna is giving her statement to Martin, a puffed-up and somewhat testy Desmond Blain enters the room. He is accompanied by Helen, who has returned from her duties in Kendal. She has been asked to take the notes of this interview, Martin being otherwise occupied.

DI Wordsworth makes to shake Desmond's hand, changes his mind and asks him to sit down.

'We have been talking to your wife, as you know. She tells us that on the night that Joyce Todd was murdered, you were out somewhere. This is contrary to what you told us during our preliminary investigations. Can you enlighten me?'

Desmond is ready for a fight: 'Nothing surprises me anymore, do you know that? Ever since your colleagues cocked it up last time, you've been obsessed with going down the same error-strewn road. Once again, you are wrong. You have made another big mistake. Donna and I were at home all night. She will have told you that. I'm not being played for an idiot by you.'

'She has made a statement saying that you went out that night.'

'Don't be ridiculous!'

'There are a couple of other pieces of evidence that we have obtained. As you know, both you and your wife - along with twenty or so other people - volunteered DNA samples and fingerprints.'

'Volunteered! Yes, that's the word!

'A few minutes ago, I interviewed both you and your wife. Both of you told me that you did not know Darren Melling.'

'That's true.'

'Darren Melling used to come into ForGiving every week, sometimes on two or three occasions, and he chatted both to your wife and to you.'

'That's news to me! Maybe I did see him, but I don't know the names of all our customers.'

'You appear to know this particular customer well.'

'What do you mean?'

Max looks at Desmond and decides that it is time to ratchet things up to the next level.

'I told you that we have a number of pieces of evidence that show that both Joyce Todd and Darren Melling were murdered. We also believe that they might have been murdered on the same night.'

'Even if they were, that's nothing to do with me.'

'The DNA tests that we requested came back yesterday, and this is the reason why I have called you in to speak to us.'

'DNA? I was happy to be tested. I have no connection with either of those deaths. What are you suggesting?'

Max stands, pops his head out of the door and calls for Martin. 'DC Tomlinson, please thank Mrs Blain for her assistance. When she has completed her statement, she is free to go. Please show her out, and then come in here.'

Max sits down again and looks at Desmond. 'This is perplexing. You seem to live a complicated life, sir. Where did Joyce Todd fit in to the scheme of things?'

'Nowhere. She didn't fit in anywhere. She was a volunteer at ForGiving, and that is all.'

'You said that you had never been in her house.'

'True, I haven't. I think that I told you once before that I occasionally dropped her off outside, but nothing more. I never went inside the house.'

'But we have forensic evidence that places you in that house.'

'Nonsense!'

You also said to me that you did not know Darren Melling, the man whose body was found at his house at Under Loughrigg.'

'And I don't! I know the name. He occasionally came into the shop.'

Martin comes back into the room and sits at his desk, note pad and pen at the ready. Helen smiles at him and then they both focus their attention on Desmond.

'And this is where things have become difficult, sir. Not only do we have incontrovertible evidence that you personally know Mr Melling, but your wife has made a statement to the effect that you were having a personal - a sexual relationship with him.'

'What? Me? You have nothing of the sort! A sexual relationship - with a man? You have lost the plot, completely lost it!'

'Your wife has given a statement in which she says that Darren Melling was one of a number of romantic liaisons that you have engaged in over the years.'

'Don't be ridiculous! This is harassment, you know. And your man here, taking the notes - he's a witness to all this.' Looking at Helen, he says, 'You had better start looking for another job too!'

Through the window Desmond sees his wife walking away back into the village. She does not look back.

He continues, 'I don't know why you are doing this, but you've got it entirely wrong. This is another catastrophe for you all! Can you imagine what the press will make of a second complete and absolute disaster. You'll be toast – all of you!

'I have never been in Joyce's house, and I have never - ever - had a relationship with the man you just mentioned. And for the record,' he turns towards Martin and Helen as if to emphasise the point, 'I have never had a homosexual relationship of any kind - with anyone - ever!'

'That will be for the CPS to decide. The evidence that we have so far appears to suggest otherwise, and while we are talking about evidence, I need to ask you about another matter.'

'Oh yes? More fantasies?'

'I don't think so.' Max takes a small clear plastic envelope out from one of the files on his desk. Inside the cellophane can be seen some of the notes that were written to Mickey.

'These notes apparently came from Joyce, Ms Blain.   They appear to be in her handwriting. However, it is your DNA that is all over the cards. Can you explain to me how that is?'

Desmond considers his answer. This is difficult: can he bluff his way out of it? Probably not. After all, he did write them.

'It was a joke. Yes, I wrote them. I was playing a joke on Mickey. I was going to tell him. It was for a laugh. He would have seen the funny side, he likes a laugh, Mickey.'

'I doubt if he would see the funny side - as there is no funny side. Did Joyce find out about this too?'

'What do you mean?'

'Did she find out that you were sending evil messages to one of her colleagues by forging her handwriting? You can see where this is going?'

He certainly can. Desmond sees a pile of evidence, none of which is true, but all of which is pointing to him in a most unfavourable way.

'Oh, and were you also stealing from ForGiving, and did she find out about that too? I told you that she was a store detective before coming up here. Did she find you out?'

'Ridiculous! This goes from bad to worse.'

'I don't think so. We've also looked at your bank accounts, your online transactions with 'Happy Roulette' - is that what it's called, Martin?'

'Yes sir. 'Happy Roulette.''

'it doesn't appear to have made you too happy, does it, sir?'

Desmond is silent - far too much information is coursing through his mind for him to be able to process any of it.

Max decides that enough is enough: 'I am placing you under arrest now. I will caution you and then have you taken to Kendal police station for further questioning.'

'You are going to arrest me - for what?'

'I am arresting you on suspicion of the murders of Joyce Todd and Darren Melling. You do not have to say anything, but it may harm your defence if you do not mention something ...'

The words of the caution are lost on Desmond as DC Tomlinson places the handcuffs on him. 'I have had to cuff you, sir,' Max explains. 'There is a cell here in Ambleton, and that would have been handy, but Health and Safety means that it can't be used any more for the detention of prisoners. It makes a very secure store room, though. We will take you to Kendal police station and put you before a magistrate. We are asking that you are remanded in custody so that we can question you further. Martin, is the car on its way?'

'Yes, sir. It won't be long.'

'In that case, Mr Blain, I want you to sit quietly here until the car arrives. When you get to Kendal, you will be able to inform your solicitor, or if you wish, we will appoint one for you - and then you will be formally questioned regarding your role in these two murders.'

Desmond is looking at his wrists. He has never been handcuffed before - those pink fluffy things don't count - and his overwhelming feeling is one of embarrassment. What would those women at ForGiving be thinking now? What would his new friend the ambassador's wife be thinking if she chanced to see him? Sad, alone - his wife clip-clopping her way back into the village?

All this spurs him on to mount yet another attack on these stupid people who are digging such a pit for themselves.

'You are all completely mad! Are you aware how unprofessionally you are behaving? Can your force really face a second fiasco? Not able to find the real murderer, you are making this up as you go along! These murders are nothing to do with me; you are digging yourselves into a deeper hole, that's all!

'If you let me go now, I'll accept your apology. But if you keep me like this, I promise you that you will regret it for the rest of your lives!'

Max says, 'Maybe you would like me to contact your solicitor now? We can arrange for him to meet you at Kendal police station. You have the right to legal representation, and you do need it.'

Desmond doesn't respond; his mind is racing, and Max can see in his eyes and in his demeanour, that although he is trying to make sense of what is happening to him, he can't. His mind is like a car stuck in the mud: revving and overheating, but making no progress - not moving anywhere.

Max decides to move matters along, 'Martin, call Kendal now and arrange for the duty solicitor to come and speak to Mr Blain sometime this afternoon.'

'Yes, sir.' Martin stands and moves to the door, taking his papers with him. 'I'll work on these notes too. We'll have Mrs Blain's statement, and maybe Mr Blain's later today?'

Max looks at Martin and says, 'Good idea.' Turning to Desmond, he says, 'Do you wish to make a statement now? It would save time for us all.'

There is still some fight left in Desmond, although the last few moments have deflated him. He's worried that there now might be some substance in what the police officers have been saying. The nightmare that is now playing out in real time - dread: way beyond the four-in-the-morning panic attacks that have always assailed him - now has its own momentum, and he is losing control of the few choices that he once had. Donna has moved on and left him to it; the police seem to have a plausible case against him. What exactly has Donna said?

Homosexual? What is that all about? Donna knows he's not gay. They've been together for over forty years, for God's sake. She would have found out by now, wouldn't she? She knows he is - has always been - straight down the line. A few kinks, yes, but hetero kinks. He looks at Max who is making some notes of his own.

'You used the word 'incontrovertible' before.'

'Yes.'

'You haven't told me what it is.'

'No.'

'Why?'

'I want to put it to you in the presence of your solicitor.'

'I'd like to know now, please.'

'It would be better for you to wait until you have legal representation. You will then be able to make an informed choice as to your next steps.'

'Bollocks to that! If you have something against me, I want to know what it is. And I want to know before I get into any police car.'

Desmond has caught Max's eye and they are both in a kind of stand-off as Martin comes back into the room.

'The car will be here in two minutes, sir.'

'Ok,' Max replies. 'Martin - DC Tomlinson. Will you read the notes relating to the evidence that we found?'

'Tell me what you have. Keep it simple.' Desmond is not angry and now Max sees, possibly for the first time, his resolve. He's being assertive, not aggressive, and Max must admit that he is quite impressed.

He decides that it is he who should explain. 'In Joyce Todd's house, your DNA was found on a paper tissue. It was next to the body, slightly under it.'

'Under the body? Rubbish! And why wasn't that 'evidence' picked up before?'

'As you know, quite a few things were not 'picked up' in the way that they should have been. We got our first suspect quite quickly, and some things that should have been done - weren't.'

'I came into this investigation and started again from the beginning. This new evidence has only now been processed. That should have happened before. If we had done our work properly, we might have had you in here some time ago.'

'And you are doing your work properly now? I don't think so!' The contempt in the man's voice tempts Max to want to punch him on the nose.

'With regard to Darren Melling,' he continues, keeping it professional, and controlling the urge, 'the piece of evidence that links you to him is somewhat personal.'

'Personal? Spit it out, man!'

On another occasion, that remark might have forced a grim smile out of Max, but he does not allow it to deflect him from the seriousness of the occasion.

'A forensic examination of the body of Darren Melling found a hair in his mouth - a pubic hair. One of your pubic hairs. Do you have any idea of how it might have got there?'

'Apart from you people putting it there in a desperate attempt to get a conviction? No, I have not! The whole idea is ludicrous.

'You can't find the murderer, even if there is one, so you have concocted evidence against me. You are going to have to do better than this. This is not a case, it's a stitch-up, and you know it!'

Max is confident enough to say, 'Our evidence that you were present at both murders is convincing and that, along with the statement from your wife, is enough to put before the CPS. We do have a case, and we'll continue this discussion more formally when we question you back at Kendal police station. There are more matters that we need to discuss.'

'There is nothing that will stand up in court!'

Max replies, 'Not for me to say, is it? We collect the evidence - and there seems to be plenty of it.

'As I mentioned, we will be talking about your bank accounts - and your serious online gambling habit.

That adds to our case - motivation for what you did. It's not complete yet; we have many things to follow up on, but I believe that our case will be that Joyce caught you fiddling at ForGiving and she had to be silenced. The other victim was a personal matter, and although we haven't yet found a connection to the death of Ms Todd, your wife has been very helpful.'

'She's making all that up! It's all completely false? Did you put her up to that?'

Max allows himself a smile. 'That information was offered to us by your wife. It surprised us too, but it does help to explain things.

'And, of course, the audit that we have requested is going to throw up some interesting evidence too.'

Martin intervenes, 'Mrs Blain has volunteered the information that the scam you were running at ForGiving was something to do with falsifying price tags. She says that she has those tags, and that she will make them available to us.'

Max looks at Desmond, reading his body language. The man's bluster has evaporated. He is defeated; there's no resistance left.

'Yes,' Max says to himself, 'I think we have nailed it this time.' He looks out of the window and Desmond says, 'And here is your car, perfect timing!

'Martin, escort Mr Blain to the car. Go with him to Kendal to have him processed. Let me know if there is any problem about having him remanded.'

And then to Desmond, 'You'll be remanded in custody to either Lancaster or Preston prison, but tonight we will keep you in Kendal. It's an opportunity to get used to the comforts of a cell, but also for you to enjoy your first prison cuisine - although we buy in at the Kendal nick. You like MacDonald's? Or are you a KFC man? I hope that we don't disappoint you too much.'

***

'So, all in all, a good result, Max. Well done!'

'Thank you, sir. I think it was. Possibly better than we could have expected.'

'You are right, there. Much better! We are all grateful to you.'

The chief constable's obvious relief indicates just how important the outcome of this Ambleton project has been. The chief, in particular, was under huge pressure given the fiasco of the first investigation. As he and Max enjoy a quiet cup of coffee, the local TV station has just congratulated the force on getting it right this time.

'I had my doubts,' replies Max. 'We'd messed things up so badly the first time that I wasn't at all sure that we could get it right.'

'Yes,' says the chief. 'I don't want to have to wade through that kind of mess again. Trial by television is not my favourite blood sport.'

'If I may say so sir, you handled that side of things very well. Being straightforward about the errors that we had made, rather than making excuses for them.'

'Mmm, I'd like to say that was a strategic decision, a deliberate ploy, but I'm not entirely sure that it was. Things moved at such a pace that we simply had to react to them. I would have preferred a more strategic approach, but it was not to be. It was our fault; we shot ourselves in the foot first time around. However, we did get our man, and he'll be away for a very long time.'

'He's nearly seventy now sir. He probably won't come out.'

'Good! That's how it should be!' The chief showing an aspect of his personality that Max hasn't seen before. 'Life should mean life. Awful man, from what I can gather.'

'There was something - creepy about him right from the start. He's been kept afloat for years by his wife. She was almost a carer for him, keeping him out of trouble.'

'But failing.'

'Yes sir, but failing. All this will be a great relief to her.'

'Look on the bright side.'

'Is there one?'

'In police work? No. No bright side - but your young DC found love, didn't he?'

'He did, yes.'

'So maybe that's a bright side. It's something for us to grasp on to - small mercies.'

The chief constable re-fills Max's coffee. 'You did a great job, Max - very skilful. And it was noticed! We are promoting you with immediate effect.'

'Promotion?'

'Oh yes, Max. Don't say no. We want you on the senior management team as soon as possible. And your man, Tomlinson? We've agreed to his transfer request, so he should be a happy chappie too. Too early for a promotion, but he's got a great career ahead of if he applies himself.'

'He'll appreciate that, sir. And I think that the Lakes will suit him very well.'

'He'll still be on your team. I'll want you to keep the relationship going in a formal way, so that we can have half a chance of snuffing out any more cockups in the future.

'The last few months have not been easy, but I think that we are getting ourselves on to a more even keel. And much of that is down to your good, solid police work. Thanks again. Now you can go. I have some real policing to do now. Council committee in half an hour.'

The chief smiles a rueful smile, shakes Max's hand and sees him to the door.

***

Desmond Blain was convicted of the murders of Joyce Todd and Darren Melling on the unanimous verdict of the jury. He was given two life sentences to run concurrently.

Max and DC Tomlinson, along with Helen Lang, their assistant, had collected sufficient evidence to convince the CPS of their case. But it was the surprisingly helpful testimony of Desmond's wife Donna, that seemed to move the jury towards its unanimous verdict. On hearing his wife testify, Desmond, already having descended into a deep depression while on remand, gave up any hope of an acquittal. He almost believed what Donna was saying, so convincing was the testimony she gave.

***

Back in Ambleton, Max, Martin and Helen meet for the final time to clear out of their temporary office and complete the mountain of paperwork in order to sign off the case. They sit together for one last cup of coffee. As a parting gift, Max has brought Danish pastries from the local bakery, The Apple Pie, and he is now thumbing through one of the national papers that has been following the case very carefully.

'Here, listen to this: *The two hours that Donna Blain spent in the witness box detailing her years of abuse and neglect at the hands of a gay serial philanderer, produced a masterpiece of controlled anguish. The decorous way in which she managed almost, but not quite, to control her tears, created the exact context that was needed to explain why her husband felt forced into the actions that he took.'*

'And there's more: *'She spoke more in sorrow than in anger of the years of what she called her humiliation. The jury, as well as the rest of the courtroom, understood exactly how she felt, their empathy expressed by their concerned expressions and the shedding of occasional tears.*

She should not have had to go through this, they seemed to say. We are on your side. This man is an evil man, and despite your brave attempts to keep him safe through many challenges, it was no fault of yours that he committed these unspeakable acts.''

Martin interrupts, 'They don't actually believe her, do they?'

'It seems they do,' replies Max. 'A bit tough on Desmond! I thought he was more a loser - out of his depth with a woman he couldn't handle.

'It will go to appeal, so we had better make sure that we complete all this work correctly.'

Do you think that we have got it wrong?'

'No, I don't think so. I think we got it right. Why? Do you?'

Breaking into the short silence that follows the question, Max says, 'In any event, the Appeal Court will look at all the evidence again. We've done our bit; we've secured the conviction.'

Martin agrees, 'Yes, and the CPS were up for it too.   However, I would like to know where was his defence in all this? Why was Donna's testimony not tested more thoroughly in cross examination?'

'I think that the answer is simple: Desmond changed his plea to 'guilty'. All fight gone, his soulmate about to betray him, he was prepared and content to accept what became inevitable.'

As the three colleagues enjoy their Danish pastries and a second coffee, the conversation drifts away from the case, and even past the need to complete all the paperwork. It focuses on the plans that Helen and Martin have begun to make now that Martin has been granted his transfer.

They are going to get a place together in the Lakes, and maybe after a few months they will think of getting married. 'I'm a conventional girl at heart, and my mum and dad would love to see me in a wedding dress!'

***

The guilty plea accepted; matters had naturally moved on swiftly. After the judge handed down the two mandatory life sentences, Desmond politely thanked the judge, looked around the courtroom to see if he could catch sight of his Donna, and not being able to see her, lowered his gaze - and was gone.

Donna wasn't there. In retrospect, that was something she later would regret. She could have been briefly proud of him for a short while, as his dignified bearing impressed everyone present.

But no, Donna had a new project that now occupied her waking hours; she had not wasted a moment.

The man she called 'Option Two', Darren - the same man whom she unfortunately had to murder, but that's ok because Desmond had taken the blame for that – and it was 'water under the bridge'.

This Darren seems to have surprised her more in death than he ever was going to do in life. A social scene of playing bowls and going out to masonic evenings would probably have lost its charm quite quickly. Donna was very aware of that, and was relieved that ultimately, she did not have to keep any of the promises that she had made to Darren, the man she still thought of as 'Option Two'.

But evidently, Darren thought of nothing else but his Donna. He had promised her that he would look after her - and look after her, he did!

A short while after the inquest into his death, and the finality of Desmond's trial and subsequent sentence, Donna was surprised to receive a letter from a solicitor's office in Blackpool.

Darren's recently drawn-up will had made Donna his sole beneficiary. As well as the Ambleton house, there was a small portfolio of shares plus the proceeds of the sale of his three shops - all of which he had owned outright. Overnight, Donna was wealthy; a woman of property with money to spend, places to go - and with nobody to hold her back.

She would have loved to have been able to share that good fortune with Desmond, but that sentimentality was quickly kicked into the long grass as she contemplated the tremendous new possibilities that were now on offer.

Donna knows exactly what she will do next: it will be a cruise! Money makes money, and she will invest a little of her new riches immediately. If it works, it works. If not, it's back to her new home in Ambleton - but without the James Last soundtrack. Donna's first cruise will take her to the Caribbean, the Mediterranean or possibly even Dubai - to wherever she can get herself a real man. She is looking for a wealthy - and we are talking of a seriously wealthy man, perhaps a widower with an eye for the slightly more mature woman with a winning personality? Donna has arrived!

The End

In his day job, Tony Hunt is a management consultant. He writes and presents business-related seminars, many of which are now available online. He and his wife live in a quiet valley in the Lake District, their five children now making their own way in the world.

Printed in Great Britain
by Amazon

20216070R00082